Christmas Wedding Bell BRIDES

Christmas
Wedding Bell
BRIDES

Hearts Ring True with Love in
Four Historical Romances

AMANDA CABOT, MARY CONNEALY,
MIRALEE FERRELL, DAVALYNN SPENCER

BARBOUR BOOKS
An Imprint of Barbour Publishing, Inc.

ISBN 978-1-63058-936-3

All scripture quotations are taken from the King James Version of the Bible.

This book is a work of fiction. Names, characters, places, and incidents are either products of the author's imagination or used fictitiously. Any similarity to actual people, organizations, and/or events is purely coincidental.

Published by Barbour Books, an imprint of Barbour Publishing, Inc., P.O. Box 719, Uhrichsville, Ohio 44683,
www.barbourbooks.com

Our mission is to publish and distribute inspirational products offering exceptional value and biblical encouragement to the masses.

Member of the
Evangelical Christian
Publishers Association

Printed in the United States of America.

The Christmas Star Bride
by Amanda Cabot

"The Lord redeemeth the soul of his servants, and none of them that trust in him shall be desolate."

PSALM 34:22

Chapter 1

There had to be a way. Esther Hathaway punched the dough with more force than normal. A good kneading was just what her trademark pumpernickel needed. She could—and would—provide that. If only she could find what *she* needed as easily.

Four weeks from today was Christmas, the day to celebrate the most wonderful gift ever given. It was also the day her niece would become Mrs. Lieutenant Michael Porter. Esther sighed as she gave the dough another punch. Susan's dress was almost finished. They had chosen the cake Esther would bake. Michael's parents had their train tickets and hotel reservations. Everything was on schedule with one exception: Esther's gift.

With the kneading complete, she slid the ball of dough into the lightly greased bowl and covered it with a towel to let it rise. The sweet white dough that would become cinnamon rolls for her early morning customers had already completed its first rising and was ready to be rolled out and filled with the rich butter and cinnamon filling.

Esther's hands moved mechanically, performing the tasks they did each morning, while her mind focused on the problem that had wakened her in the middle of the night. Susan claimed it didn't matter, but it did. Four generations of Hathaway women had had their Christmas stars, and Susan would, too.

A smile crossed Esther's face as she thought of the stars, now carefully wrapped in soft flannel, waiting for their annual unveiling and placement on the tree. Each was as different as the happy brides and grooms whose portraits were highlighted by the star-shaped frames: Esther's great-grandparents, her grandparents, her own parents, and her sister and brother-in-law. Having each couple immortalized in a Christmas ornament had become a Hathaway family tradition.

Esther, of course, had no star-shaped portrait to display on the mantel or hang on the tree. Her hopes for that had died on the blood-soaked fields of Gettysburg more than twenty years before, but Susan—the niece she loved as dearly as if she were her daughter—would carry on the tradition. If only

Esther could find a suitable artist.

Once the filling had been spread over the dough, she lifted one of the long edges and began to form it into a log that would then be cut into individual pieces and baked in one of the large, round cake tins that did double duty for cinnamon rolls.

Esther's smile turned into a frown as she thought of her search for someone capable of painting Susan and Michael's portrait. Quality. That's what she sought. When she'd taken over running the bakery, she had insisted on using nothing but the highest quality ingredients and the best pans she could find. Susan's portrait deserved the same high quality.

Esther had interviewed every portrait painter in Cheyenne, but none of them had been right. Some were too busy to take on her commission. Others lacked the talent she sought. Still others admitted they'd never painted a miniature. Though they were willing to try, Esther wasn't willing to take a chance on failure. She had found the perfect frame, a simple gold star, the only embellishment being Susan and Michael's initials engraved in each point. Now she needed an artist.

Bowing her head, Esther sent a prayer heavenward. Though she knew the good Lord had many more important things to do, she prayed that He'd send her the painter she sought. There was no answer. Of course not. It was silly to have expected an artist to knock on her door this early in the morning. She would wait.

Once the rolls were in the oven, Esther poured herself a cup of coffee and retrieved the morning paper from the front step. Settling into a chair at the kitchen table, she began to peruse the news, turning the pages slowly as she learned what had happened in Cheyenne yesterday and what events were planned for today.

Her gaze stopped and her eyes widened. The ad was so small that Esther almost missed it, but there it was, buried deep inside the paper. *Jeremy Snyder, artist. Portraits, landscapes, oils, watercolors.*

Her heart singing with happiness, she reached for a piece of stationery and an envelope. This was no coincidence. God had answered her prayers.

❧

Cheyenne was a fine city, Jeremy Snyder reflected as he headed past the train depot on Fifteenth Street. Some might complain about the noise when an iron horse chugged and whistled its way to the depot, but Jeremy wasn't one of them. He recognized the trains for what they were: the lifeblood of the city. Thanks to President Lincoln's vision of a transcontinental railroad and the Union Pacific's part in turning that vision into reality, Cheyenne existed.

Jeremy crossed Hill Street. Just one more block and he'd be able to rest his legs. Though the doctors had told him that walking was good for him, even after more than two decades it remained a painful experience if he went too far or too quickly. He'd done both today, searching for work.

Other end-of-the-rails towns had disappeared, but Cheyenne had flourished. In less than twenty years, it had grown from a rough-and-tumble tent town to one of the wealthiest cities in the country. That was why Jeremy had come. He'd reasoned that all those cattle baron millionaires would want family portraits or pretty landscapes to hang on their walls. He'd been right. They did want art work, but not from an itinerant painter like him. They could afford artists who'd gathered a following in the East. Some had even commissioned work from famous European painters.

Jeremy winced as pain radiated up his left leg, but the pain was not only physical. As much as he enjoyed living in Cheyenne, if he didn't get work soon, he'd have to move on. Though he'd hoped to stay until spring, that was beginning to seem unrealistic. The boardinghouse where he stayed was one of the cheapest in town, and he'd arranged to eat dinner only three nights a week to save money. But even with those economies, his small reserve would soon be depleted, and he'd have no choice but to leave.

He climbed the five steps leading to his boarding-house, deliberately ignoring the peeling paint and the squeaking boards beneath his feet. At least the roof did not leak, and his room had enough light that he could work there. . .if he had a commission. Lately all he'd been able to afford to paint had been watercolor landscapes. Though they filled his heart with joy, they did nothing to fill an empty stomach.

"Mr. Snyder." As Jeremy entered the boarding-house, his landlady emerged from the kitchen, an envelope in her hand. "This just came for you."

It was probably rude, but Jeremy ripped the envelope open and withdrew the single sheet of paper, his eyes scanning the few words. His heart began to thud, and he grinned at the kindly woman. "Thank you, Mrs. Tyson."

"Is it work for you?"

"I hope so."

Back in his room, Jeremy buffed his shoes, then studied his reflection in the small mirror over the bureau. No one would call him handsome, but at forty, that was no longer important. What mattered was what he was able to create with brushes and paint. He pulled his leather case from under the bed, trying to decide which items to take. Since Miss Hathaway hadn't specified whether she wanted oil or watercolor for her niece's portrait, Jeremy included a watercolor landscape along with the oil portrait of his father that he'd done from memory and the miniature of his mother.

Sitting on the one chair the room boasted, he tightened the straps that held his left foot in place. Wood didn't flex like flesh and sinews, but at least it allowed him to walk without crutches or a cane. There was nothing he could do about the limp. That was a permanent reminder of what had happened at Antietam, but it was also a reminder that he'd been fortunate. He had lived, and now, if Miss Esther Hathaway liked Jeremy's work, he would be able to spend Christmas in Cheyenne.

Mindful of the leg that protested each step, he walked slowly east. Instead of retracing his steps, this time he took Sixteenth Street, heading for the Mitchell-Hathaway Bakery on the corner of Sixteenth and Central. Jeremy had passed it numerous times on his walks through the city and had been enticed by the delicious aromas that wafted through the air each time the door opened, but he'd never been inside. The few commissions he'd obtained had barely covered room and board and the cost of supplies. There'd been nothing left for treats.

There it was, a small brick building on the southeast corner, facing Central. One plate-glass window held a display of tempting baked goods, while the other revealed four round tables that encouraged customers to enjoy a cup of coffee or tea with a pastry. Jeremy saw a second door on the Sixteenth Street side and suspected it led to the proprietor's living quarters. He'd been told that many shopkeepers lived either behind or on top of their establishments.

As Jeremy opened the front door, he was assailed by the smell of freshly baked bread and pastries, and his mouth began to water. He took another step inside, carefully closing the door behind him, thankful there were no customers to hear the rumbling of his stomach. Fixing a smile on his face, he turned. An instant later the smile froze and Jeremy felt the blood drain from his face. Instinctively, he gripped the doorframe to keep his legs from collapsing.

It couldn't be. He blinked once, twice, then a third time to clear his vision, but nothing changed. There was no mistaking that light brown hair, those clear blue eyes, and the patrician features that had haunted his memory for so many years.

"Diana, what on earth are you doing here?"

Chapter 2

Esther stared at the man who was looking at her with such horror in his eyes. Close to six-feet tall, he had medium brown hair with only a few strands of gray, and brown eyes that under other circumstances might have been warm. His features were regular, almost handsome; his clothing well made; his shoes freshly polished. He might have been a customer, but the leather portfolio he held in his left hand told Esther otherwise. Unless she was sorely mistaken, this was Jeremy Snyder, her last hope for Susan's portrait.

She took a step forward, seeking to defuse his tension by introducing herself. She wouldn't ask about Diana. Indeed, she would not. That would be unspeakably rude. "I'm Esther Hathaway," she said with the warmest smile she could muster, "and I suspect you're Mr. Snyder." Before she realized what was happening, the question slipped out. "Who is Diana?"

So much for good intentions.

The muscles in Mr. Snyder's cheek twitched as if he were trying to keep from shouting, but his voice was level as he said, "No one important."

It was a lie. Esther recognized the expression in his eyes. The shock had disappeared, only to be replaced by sorrow and longing. It was the same expression she'd seen in the mirror too many mornings, but there was more. Mr. Snyder's face had the pinched, gray look of a man who hasn't eaten well. Esther had seen that look on countless faces as men made their way home after the war. The Union might have won, but the soldiers who'd filed through town had shown no sign of celebration.

"Please have a seat, Mr. Snyder." Esther gestured toward one of the four tables that filled the right side of the store. "I'll be with you in a moment."

Fortunately this was a quiet time at the bakery, and with no customers to wait on, she could devote her attention to the man who might be the painter she sought. A slight shuffling sound made Esther glance behind her as she walked toward the kitchen, and she realized that Mr. Snyder was limping. Hungry and lame. The poor, poor man.

As she sliced and buttered bread, Esther wished she had something more substantial to offer him, but there was nothing left from her midday meal. Fortunately, two cinnamon rolls remained. She placed them on a separate plate, filled a mug with coffee, then positioned everything on a tray.

"I thought that while I was studying samples of your work, you could sample mine," she said as she arranged the plates and mug in front of him.

Though his eyes brightened momentarily, Mr. Snyder shook his head. "This isn't necessary, ma'am."

"Oh, but it is," she countered. "I can tell a lot about a man from his reaction to food. I insist."

He nodded slowly before opening his portfolio and extracting three framed pictures. "I wasn't certain whether you wanted oil or watercolors," he explained as he laid them in front of her.

Esther's eyes widened at the sight of a landscape, a man's formal portrait, and a more casual painting of a woman. "I had thought oil," she said as she picked up the watercolor landscape, "but this is magnificent. The flowers look so real I want to pick them. It's excellent work, Mr. Snyder."

"And this is the best pumpernickel I've ever eaten. There's something unique about it—a hint of coffee, perhaps?"

Esther didn't bother to mask her surprise. "You're the first person to identify it."

He shrugged as if it were of no account. "I've drunk a lot of coffee over the years, and I've learned to recognize good brews." Raising his mug in a toast, he added, "This is one of the best."

It was a simple compliment, no reason for color to rise to her cheeks, yet Esther's face warmed at the praise. To hide her confusion, she lowered her head and studied the three paintings. Each was wonderful in its own way. There was no question about it: Jeremy Snyder was the man she wanted to paint Susan and Michael's portrait.

Fearing that he might stop eating if she spoke again, Esther kept her eyes focused on the miniature of a woman she suspected was the artist's mother, waiting until he'd finished the last bite of cinnamon roll before she spoke.

"These are exactly what I was looking for. Mr. Snyder, you're the answer to my prayers."

∽

"That's the first time anyone's called me that." Jeremy took another sip of coffee, as much to avoid having to look at the woman who sat on the opposite side of the table as to wash down the last bite of that incredibly delicious cinnamon roll. She didn't sound like Diana. Her voice was firmer, a bit lower pitched than Diana's, but there was no denying the resemblance. This woman could be Diana's twin, and that hurt. Every time he looked at Miss Esther Hathaway, memories threatened to choke him.

"Tell me more about this portrait you want me to paint." Though he had every intention of refusing the commission, Jeremy had eaten the woman's food. He owed her at least a few minutes' consideration. And the truth was, other than Miss Hathaway's unfortunate resemblance to Diana, he was enjoying being here.

The bakery was warm, clean, and filled with tantalizing aromas. A pressed-tin ceiling complemented the pale blue walls and the dark wooden floors. The tables were made of a lighter shade of wood than the floor, the chair cushions a deeper blue than the walls. Though the room was not overtly feminine, Jeremy suspected it appealed to a mostly female clientele.

"I'll do more than tell you," Miss Hathaway said in response to his request. "I'll show you."

She returned from the back of the bakery a minute later, a large flannel package in her hands. Unwrapping it carefully, she withdrew four star-shaped frames and laid them on the table. To Jeremy's surprise, though he'd expected each to hold a woman's portrait, two people had their likenesses painted in each one.

"It's a family tradition," Miss Hathaway continued, "to have the bride and groom's portrait painted for their first Christmas together. My niece will be married on Christmas Day, and this will be my gift to her." The woman who looked so much like Diana gazed directly at Jeremy, not bothering to hide the eagerness in her expression. "Will you do it, Mr. Snyder?"

I can't. The words almost escaped his lips, but then he reconsidered. As painful as it would be to spend days in the company of a woman who looked so much like Diana, there was no denying that he needed the money. He needed to be practical.

Jeremy nodded slowly. "My fee for a miniature portrait is. . ." As he quoted a figure, he studied Miss Hathaway, his eyes cataloging the simple gray dress that skimmed her curves, the white collar and cuffs giving it a festive look without seeming too fancy for a shopkeeper. Though she was as beautiful as Diana, Jeremy suspected that Miss Hathaway deliberately underplayed her looks, perhaps not wanting to compete with her customers.

"You're selling yourself short, Mr. Snyder," she said with a small smile. "The other artists I've considered would have charged considerably more than that and for only one portrait. Since you'll be painting two people, it seems only fair to pay you twice that amount."

Diana would never have said anything like that, but then again, Diana would not have thought to offer a hungry man food.

"I'm not looking for charity."

Miss Hathaway gave him a piercing look. "I didn't think you were. I'm looking for excellence, and I'm willing to pay well to ensure I receive it. Now, do we have a deal, Mr. Snyder?"

There was a challenge in her voice. It was almost as if she'd read his doubts and was daring him to conquer them. They'd only just met. The woman had no way of knowing that Jeremy Snyder was not one to back down from a challenge, and yet. . .

More intrigued than he'd thought possible, Jeremy nodded. "We do."

⚬⚭⚬

"I tell you, Susan, the man is the answer to my prayers." It was several hours later, and Esther and her niece were seated at the kitchen table, their supper laid out before them. Though many shopkeepers had totally separate living quarters, when Esther's sister, Lydia, and Daniel had built the bakery, they'd seen no need for two kitchens. The apartment had two bedrooms and a sitting room but shared the bakery's kitchen. That arrangement had worked for Esther's sister and brother-in-law, and she'd seen no need to change it.

"Mr. Snyder's work is outstanding." Esther gazed at the girl who'd inherited her father's dark brown hair and eyes but her mother's delicate features, wishing Lydia and Daniel were here to share the joy of Susan's wedding plans. "You and Michael will be proud of your portrait."

Susan smiled as she buttered a piece of rye bread. "I'm glad you found him. I know I told you it didn't matter if Michael and I didn't have our star, but. . ."

"You really wanted it." Esther finished the sentence.

Blinking in surprise, Susan stared at her. "How did you know?"

"I've lived with you for the past ten years. I'd like to think I've learned a bit about you in that time." It had been a joy and at times a trial, watching Susan change from the bewildered eight-year-old whose parents had died of a cholera epidemic into a poised young woman of eighteen, but Esther did not regret a single moment.

Susan's smile softened. "Then you also know that as much as I'm looking forward to being Michael's wife, I hate the idea of leaving you." She reached across the table and touched Esther's hand. "Won't you reconsider? Michael and I want you to live with us."

Trying not to sigh at the fact that this was far

from the first time Susan had raised the subject, Esther shook her head. "I appreciate the offer. You know I do. But I don't want to give up the bakery. People depend on it." Perhaps it was wrong, but Esther couldn't help being proud of the way she turned her sister and brother-in-law's struggling enterprise into one of the most successful bakeries in Wyoming's capitol.

"There are other bakeries in Cheyenne."

"But none that feed the hungry." Knowing that it was sometimes the only food they'd have, at the close of each day, Esther took bread to the boarding houses and cheap hotels where the poorest stayed.

"I know others might not consider it a mission, but I believe I'm doing God's will. I can feel His approval in the way He's blessed me with a home of my own and you to love."

Susan had no way of knowing how important that home was to Esther. Esther had lived with her parents, caring for them until their deaths ten years ago, and then she'd moved to Cheyenne to live with Lydia and her husband.

Though she would have given anything to have had Lydia and Daniel survive the cholera and be able to raise Susan to adulthood, Esther could not deny that she had flourished in the ten years since their deaths. Forced to make her living, she'd discovered that she had a flair for both baking and attracting customers. And for the first time in her life, she had a home that was hers and hers alone. A home and independence. She couldn't—she wouldn't—give that up.

"This is my place," she said softly. "I can't leave."

Chapter 3

They were an attractive couple. Jeremy took a step to the right, studying the subjects of his next painting. Michael's golden-blond hair and blue eyes provided a pleasing contrast to Susan's darker coloring, while her yellow dress shone against the dark blue of his uniform. But what impressed Jeremy the most and what he planned to capture in their portrait was the love they shared. He took another step, wanting to see them from every angle. That love was evident in the way their smiles softened when they looked at each other and the way Michael kept Susan's hand clasped in his.

Jeremy paused, wondering whether he and Diana had been so deeply in love before the war. Though he wanted to believe they had, the way their love had ended said otherwise. But there was no point in dwelling on that, even less in envying this young couple their happiness and their bright future. While it seemed unlikely, it was still possible that God's plans for Jeremy included a wife and the kind of happiness Michael and Susan shared.

In the meantime, he had work to do. Jeremy settled onto a stool and began to sketch.

He'd been sketching for the better part of an hour when the clock chimed and Michael rose. "I'm sorry, Mr. Snyder," the young man said, his voice ringing with regret, "but I need to return to the fort."

Trying not to smile at the realization that Michael's regret was over leaving his fiancée rather than the portrait session, Jeremy nodded. "That's not a problem. Miss Hathaway explained your schedule. I've spent most of today making sketches of you. Those will be the foundation. I can fill in the details after I've finished Susan's portrait."

The truth was, Jeremy did not need to have his subject in front of him when he painted a portrait. Once he'd made the preliminary sketches, he could work from them, but since most people were accustomed to posing while the artist painted, he continued with what was almost a charade.

As Susan rose to accompany Michael to the door, Esther approached the corner of the store where Jeremy had set up his easel. Esther. Jeremy smiled. He wasn't sure when it had happened, but he'd ceased to think of her as Miss Hathaway. Of course, he wouldn't presume to address her that way, but in his mind she was Esther.

"Are you certain it's all right to work here in the main room?" She'd removed one of the tables to give Jeremy space for his equipment and the high stools that Michael and Susan had used. "Our sitting room is more private, but it just wouldn't be proper. This way Susan is chaperoned."

Esther smiled, a sweet smile that made Jeremy pause. While it was true that she resembled Diana, their smiles were not at all alike.

"I have to confess that I had a mercenary motive, too," Esther said with another smile. "I thought having you here would be good for business."

"Yours or mine?" Though he'd been in the bakery for less than two hours, Jeremy had noticed that several people had lingered to watch him. They'd bought a cup of coffee or tea and a cookie or pastry to give them a reason for sitting at one of the tables.

Esther's smile broadened. "To be honest, both. I can't compete with the variety of goods Mr. Ellis's Bakery and Confectionary offers, but at this point, I run the only bakery in Cheyenne with its own artist-in-residence."

Though she looked at the easel, she made no comment. Jeremy appreciated that. Preliminary sketches were exactly that: preliminary.

"I haven't had additional customers today, but

some of those who've come have stayed longer and spent more money than usual. Monday will be different, because word will have spread. That'll be good for me."

Jeremy grinned. "And it's free advertising for me."

"Exactly. I wouldn't be surprised if you got several commissions in the next few days."

"I won't complain if that happens." This could be the boost his career needed, a way to stay in Cheyenne until spring, maybe even longer. "I appreciate your help, Miss Hathaway."

Those lovely blue eyes twinkled with what appeared to be amusement. "We're going to be seeing a lot of each other over the next month. Please call me Esther."

Jeremy blinked in surprise. The woman was amazing. Had she read his mind and known that he no longer appreciated the formality society demanded?

"I'd like that. . .Esther."

◦∞◦

Esther bit the inside of her cheek as she tried to control her reaction. It was silly how the sound of her name on Jeremy's lips made her feel all tingly inside. The last time she'd felt that way had been before the war, and that had been a long time ago. She was no longer a girl of less than twenty pledging her love to her dearest friend; now she was a confirmed spinster with a business to run.

As Susan returned to her stool, her smile a little less bright now that Michael was no longer with her, Esther returned to the kitchen to prepare a tray with coffee and cookies. She didn't want to embarrass the man, and so she'd decided to wait until tomorrow to add a sandwich or two to the plate. She had it all planned, how she'd claim that she'd cooked too much beef and that she was afraid it might spoil. Always a gentleman, Jeremy wouldn't refuse to eat it.

"I thought you might like a break," Esther said a few minutes later as she placed the tray on the empty table next to Jeremy's easel and darted a glance at his foot.

Though Esther had always thought artists stood while they painted, Jeremy perched on a stool, undoubtedly to rest his leg. She wouldn't ask about the limp, but she'd studied the way he walked and sat and had decided that he had lost his left foot. The wooden replacement allowed him to walk, but since it did not flex like flesh and bones, it couldn't be comfortable to stand for long periods.

Susan rose, her expression once more eager. "Are

we done for today? I promised Pamela I'd help her choose a dress pattern."

Jeremy nodded. "I've got enough to work with tonight."

Esther raised an eyebrow. She hadn't expected him to work nights. Didn't artists need good light? Before she could ask, Susan clapped her hands like a small child.

"Good. Aunt Esther can keep you company." Susan kissed Esther's cheek and hurried to their apartment for her hat and cloak.

"I hope you like oatmeal cookies." The words sounded stilted, but somehow with the buffer of Susan removed and the store momentarily empty of customers, Esther felt awkward sitting across from Jeremy. She hadn't been alone with a man since the day Chester had donned his uniform and left for what they'd believed would be only a few months of fighting.

Jeremy took a bite of the cookie, chewed thoughtfully, then washed it down with a slug of coffee. "It's delicious," he said, his brown eyes serious as they met her gaze. "You added nutmeg as well as cinnamon, didn't you?"

Esther nodded. Perhaps it was foolish to be so pleased that this man appreciated the special touches she put into her baked goods, but Esther couldn't help it.

He finished the first cookie and reached for a second. "I noticed the bakery's name is Mitchell-Hathaway. Is Susan a part owner?"

This time Esther shook her head. "When I moved to Cheyenne, my sister and her husband were running it—Lydia and Daniel Mitchell. After they died, I took over. People kept calling me Miss Mitchell, so rather than explain every time, I decided to add my name to the sign."

"But you kept theirs, too."

Esther wondered why Jeremy was so interested in the bakery and its name. "They were the ones who started the business."

"From what I've heard, it was struggling, and you're the one who made it the success it is today."

"Who said that?" As color rose to her cheeks, Esther tried to tamp down her embarrassment. She shouldn't be blushing simply because this man had called her a success.

He shrugged. "Does it matter if it's true?"

"I suppose not. I am proud of the way the business has grown. I hadn't expected it, but it's very rewarding—and I don't mean only monetarily—to create a new recipe and watch people enjoy it. I feel as if I was called to do this."

The instant the words were out of her mouth, Esther regretted them. Why was she confiding her inner thoughts to a man who was practically a stranger? The answer came quickly: for some reason, Jeremy didn't feel like a stranger.

"Have you always been a painter?" she asked, determined to turn the focus away from herself.

A brief shake of the head was Jeremy's response. He was silent for a moment before saying, "Only since the war. Before that I was a farmer." He took another sip of coffee, and Esther suspected he was corralling his emotions. Mention of the war had that effect on many.

"The war changed my life," he said, confirming her supposition. "At night, after we'd been marching all day, men would play the harmonica or sing. I couldn't do either, so I started making sketches for them to send to their mothers or sweethearts. They liked the results, and I realized that I enjoyed sketching. It was one good thing that came out of the war."

The way he said *one* told Esther there was at least one other. "What were the others?"

"There's only one. I discovered the joy of traveling and exploring new places. Before the war, I had never been more than ten miles from my home. Now I've seen almost every part of this great country."

It was a life Esther could not imagine. She hadn't particularly enjoyed the trip from Central New York to Cheyenne, and now that she was here, she had no desire to travel farther.

"So you don't have a permanent home?" That was even more difficult to understand.

"No. I haven't yet found a place where I wanted to stay."

And she was firmly rooted in Wyoming Territory.

It didn't matter that Jeremy was the most intriguing man Esther had ever met. He was like the jackrabbit that had fascinated Susan one winter when it had apparently taken residence under one of their lilac bushes. Susan would check each morning and every afternoon when she returned from school, giggling with delight when the rabbit was still there. And then one day it had disappeared, leaving Susan feeling bereft. Like the rabbit, Jeremy was merely passing through Cheyenne and Esther's life.

Chapter 4

Five days. It had been five days since he'd met Esther, five days since his life had changed. Jeremy couldn't claim he understood the reason, but he found himself dreaming of her every night. And now he was here, in the warm, aromatic building that had become his studio as well as her bakery.

"I'm so excited about having my own home." Susan's smile turned into a grin. Though she was good about remaining motionless while Jeremy captured her likeness on canvas, the instant he lifted his brush, she began to speak, her words as effervescent as the fizzy drinks he'd enjoyed as a boy.

"Michael showed me what officers' housing is like," she continued. "Did you know that families have to move if a higher ranking person comes to the fort? Sometimes they only get a day's notice." Susan shuddered in apparent dismay. "I don't imagine that'll happen to us, though. We're going to be in one of the smallest houses at the fort. That doesn't matter, though, because it'll be ours."

To Jeremy's surprise, the corners of Susan's

mouth turned downward. "I only wish Aunt Esther was going with us."

Jeremy doubted any newlyweds really wanted company, but Susan seemed sincere. "You'll still be able to see her."

"It won't be the same. I don't know what I'd have done without her. She's been like a mother to me ever since my parents died." Susan continued talking, repeating the story Jeremy had heard about how Esther had revived the bakery at the same time that she'd adopted her orphaned niece.

"She's a remarkable woman." That must be the reason Esther dominated his thoughts. The only reason.

⌒∞⌒

"Mrs. Bradford is here for your fitting, Susan." Esther smiled at Jeremy as her niece rose from the stool, shaking her arms and legs as if to relieve a cramp. "It shouldn't take too long." Pointing to the wall that divided the bakery from her sitting room, she smiled again. "Just knock on the wall if a customer arrives."

Jeremy shrugged as he swirled the tip of his brush on the palette. "I have plenty to do. You needn't worry about me."

But she did worry about him, Esther admitted as

she followed Susan to their apartment where Mrs. Bradford waited with the wedding gown. Though she couldn't explain it, Esther dreamed about Jeremy every night. When she awakened, all she could remember were fragments, but they were enough to convince her that Jeremy Snyder's life had not been an easy one. It wasn't only his limp or the painful thinness that worried her. More important was the sadness she saw in his eyes when he didn't realize she was watching.

"You're a good Christian woman, Miss Hatha-way," Mrs. Bradford said as they waited for Susan to slip out of her daytime dress. She smoothed the hair that had once been a bright auburn but was now fading and threaded with silver and gave Esther a look that could only be called patronizing. "I admire you for taking pity on that poor man. It's such a shame that he's been afflicted with that limp, but it explains why he's not married. No woman would want to be shackled to a man like that."

How dare she say that! Esther felt her hackles rise. "You're wrong, Mrs. Bradford." What she wanted to do was slap the woman who'd insulted Jeremy, but good manners kept her hands at her side. "There is nothing pitiful about Jeremy. He's a strong man and a very talented artist. Any woman would be proud to be seen in his company."

The seamstress raised an eyebrow, her expression calculating. "Jeremy, is it? Just what is going on here?" Her tone left no doubt she thought the worst.

Esther took a deep breath, exhaling slowly as she corralled her anger. "What is going on? Simple. I've employed Jeremy"—she stressed his name—"to paint my niece's portrait, just as I've employed you to sew her gown." She stared at the woman who was one of Cheyenne's premier seamstresses. "I can see that you don't believe me. That's your prerogative, but if I hear any scurrilous gossip, you may be certain I will tell my customers that, although you are skilled with a needle, you are less skilled at minding your own business."

The woman's eyes widened, and a flush stained her cheeks. "I didn't mean I thought anything wrong was going on."

Esther let the lie slide. There was nothing to be gained by continuing the confrontation. As Susan emerged from her bedroom, Esther forced a bright smile to her face. "What do you think about adding another row of ruffles to the skirt?"

Though anger still simmered, by the time she and Susan had made a decision about the ruffles, Esther felt calm enough to face Jeremy. She hadn't wanted to do that when she feared her face would reveal her fury with the outspoken seamstress, but a quick glance in the mirror told her that her color had returned to normal.

"I wondered if you could start coming earlier, perhaps around eleven," she said as she approached Jeremy. He was cleaning his brushes, the pungent smell of turpentine mingling with the more pleasing aromas of yeast and chocolate. When he raised a questioning eyebrow, she continued. "Susan and I would like you to join us for our midday meal. That will give us an opportunity to discuss the portrait."

It was an excuse, nothing more, to ensure that he had at least one good meal a day. If it also gave her the opportunity to spend more time with him, well. . .that was an added benefit.

Curiosity turned to surprise, and Jeremy raised one eyebrow. "I can certainly arrange that, if you think it's wise." The way he phrased the acceptance made Esther suspect he'd overheard Mrs. Bradford's comments and her response through the thin walls.

"I do." Oh, that hadn't come out the way she had planned. "I do think it's wise," she amended, lest his thoughts had turned the direction hers had, to wedding vows. "Michael will come whenever he can, but you realize the army has first call on him."

Jeremy's eyes crinkled as he smiled. "That I do. And that leads me to something I wanted to discuss with you." He gestured toward his easel. "I studied the other portraits, because I know you want this one to be similar. I'd like to suggest one change, though. Their backgrounds are all plain. I wondered if you might want something different for Susan and Michael."

Esther hadn't thought about backgrounds. Her focus had been entirely on finding an artist talented enough to convey the young couple's likeness onto canvas. "What would you suggest?"

"Perhaps some aspect of Fort Russell. After all, that's where their married life will begin."

As happiness bubbled up from deep inside her, Esther gave Jeremy a warm smile. In all likelihood, the men who'd painted the other family portraits hadn't been skilled at landscapes. Jeremy was. "What a wonderful idea! That would make Susan's star even more special."

He nodded, obviously pleased by her enthusiasm. "There's only one problem. I haven't seen the fort, and I don't know which location they'd prefer."

Esther doubted either Susan or Michael did, either. "If you can wait a few days, we can all go together. I can't leave the store, so that means Sunday."

She took a shallow breath before she continued. "Would next Sunday after church and dinner be a good time for you?"

"Perfect. I'm looking forward to it."

So was she.

Chapter 5

It was the perfect day for a ride. The deep blue Wyoming sky accented by a few puffy cumulus clouds always brought a smile to Esther's face. Though at this altitude the sun made the air feel warmer than the thermometer claimed, the presence of the man at her side warmed her far more than the sun. It had been so long—half a lifetime—since she'd gone for a Sunday ride with a man.

Susan had taken the backseat, insisting that Esther sit in front with Jeremy, and though they had tried to involve her in the conversation, she had closed her eyes as if she were dozing. Esther knew it was feigned sleep. Susan was playing matchmaker, wanting her aunt to have time alone with Jeremy.

More pleased by her niece's ploy than she wanted to admit, Esther shifted slightly on the seat and gazed at the man who'd captured her imagination. They talked about everything and nothing. Jeremy told her how grateful he was to be painting in the bakery, because he already had three new commissions. Esther confided that her business had improved since he'd been there. They spoke of the weather, of the harsh beauty of the Wyoming prairie. They discussed the relative merits of pumpernickel and rye bread and the different uses for watercolors and oil paints. The one thing they did not discuss was Diana.

Esther took a deep breath, exhaling slowly as she unclenched her fists. Ever since the day she'd met Jeremy, she had known that Diana—whoever she was—was an important part of his life. While Mrs. Bradford might claim otherwise, Esther believed that Jeremy had chosen to remain unmarried, that Diana, and not his wooden foot, was the reason he was a bachelor. Though she longed to know the story, Esther wouldn't ask. That wouldn't be polite, and if there was one thing Esther had been raised to be, it was polite. But she couldn't help wanting to learn more about Diana and her role in Jeremy's life.

∽

Jeremy smiled and loosened his grip on the reins. The horses seemed content to amble along. Perhaps they recognized that he was more than content to continue riding, so long as Esther was at his side. He took a deep breath as he gazed at the woman who'd captured his thoughts. She was remarkable, the kindest person Jeremy had ever met. Look at the way she'd invited him to have dinner with her every day.

The need to discuss Susan's portrait had been only an excuse. Jeremy knew that. What Esther really wanted was to ensure that he was well fed. Perhaps he should have refused, but he hadn't, for there was nothing he'd wanted more than to spend time in Miss Esther Hathaway's company.

The food wasn't the attraction, although she was a superb cook. No, the simple fact was that he enjoyed being with Esther. He admired her quick wit, her friendly smile, the obvious love she lavished on her niece. Even more, he enjoyed the way she made him feel almost as if he were part of the family.

Perhaps he was mistaken. Perhaps this was the way she treated everyone, but Jeremy did not want to believe that. What he wanted to believe was that she had begun to harbor some of the tender feelings that welled up inside him every time he was with her, every time he thought of her.

It was too soon to ask her that, and so Jeremy posed the first question that popped into his brain. "Do many of the officers' wives visit your bakery?" Though the answer affected his plans, what he really wanted to ask was why a woman as wonderful as Esther had never married. Susan chattered about almost everything else, but that was one subject she had never mentioned, and Jeremy hadn't wanted to pry.

"A few. Why?"

For a second he wondered what Esther was saying. Then he remembered the question he'd posed. Clearing his throat, he said, "I was hoping some of them might be interested in my paintings. I thought perhaps they'd want a landscape to remind them of their time in Wyoming Territory." And if they did, he would have a little more spare cash to do some of the things he'd begun to dream of.

Esther tipped her head to the side, as if considering. "I don't know any of the wives well, so I can't predict their reaction. Why don't you bring the landscape you showed me to the store? That way we can see if they're interested."

We? Jeremy felt a bubble of hope well up deep inside him at Esther's casual use of the plural pronoun. It might mean nothing, and yet it could mean that she'd begun to feel the way he did. "I have other landscapes finished," he admitted, pleased that his voice did not betray his excitement. "Portraits are easier to sell, but landscapes are what I enjoy most."

"Then you should focus on them. Life is too short to do things you don't enjoy."

Jeremy couldn't agree more. Though part of him

wanted the ride to last forever, Fort Russell was only a few miles northwest of Cheyenne, and they soon reached it. The collection of mostly frame buildings around the diamond-shaped parade ground caught Jeremy's eye, and he could envision that as the background for the portrait, but after touring the whole fort, looking for possible sites for their portrait's background, Michael and Susan chose the house they'd share.

Though it wouldn't have been Jeremy's choice, he understood their reasons. Pulling out the folding chair Esther had insisted they bring, he began to work. While Jeremy sketched the simple building with the modest front porch and the young couple strolled along the walkways, he couldn't help noticing that Esther was deep in conversation with two women who'd come out of neighboring houses.

"You're right," the taller of the women said, her voice loud enough that Jeremy had no trouble distinguishing her words. "A painting would make a wonderful Christmas gift. I'll come into town tomorrow to see which one I like best."

"And I'll be with her." The second woman's giggle made Jeremy think she was no older than Susan. "My husband deserves one, too."

Jeremy grinned. Unless he was mistaken, Esther

Christmas Wedding Bell Brides

had just sold two of his landscapes. She was a truly remarkable woman.

⁂

"I'm so glad we went to the fort." Susan smiled as she drew the brush through her hair one last time. "My star will be the most beautiful of them all."

If there was one thing Esther could count on, it was her niece's enthusiasm. "Jeremy's very talented," she said.

"He's handsome, too. . .for an older man," Susan added, the corners of her lips turning into a grin. "Don't shake your head, Aunt Esther. I know you've noticed, and *I've* noticed the way your eyes sparkle when he's around." She started to braid her hair, then turned back to look at Esther. "I think you're harboring special feelings for him."

"Nonsense!" Esther glared at her niece. It was true Jeremy was never far from her thoughts. It was true she treasured the time they spent together. It was true she had begun to dream of a future that somehow included him. But Esther wasn't ready to admit that to Susan.

That night she dreamed of Jeremy again. The dream began the way it always did, with him walking down a deserted lane. Then it changed, and it became clear that this was no aimless strolling. His stride was purposeful, the purpose soon apparent. A beautiful woman was waiting at the end of the lane. Diana.

∞

"Who's Diana?" Taking advantage of the momentary lull between customers, Esther was sharing coffee and dried apple pie with Jeremy when the words popped out of her mouth. She hadn't intended to ask, but now that the question was in the air, she did not regret it.

Jeremy did. That was apparent from the way he shook his head, his lips tightening and his expression darkening. He stared at the pie on his plate as if the answers were there, and Esther suspected he would not speak. Then, after a few seconds, he raised his eyes to meet her gaze. "I don't like to talk about her," he said softly, "but you deserve to know." He took a sip of coffee before continuing. "Diana is the woman I wanted to marry."

Is, present tense. That meant she was still alive. "What happened?"

Gesturing toward his left foot, Jeremy scowled. "Antietam is what happened. I lost my foot and my fiancée the same day. I just didn't know it at the time."

He ran his finger over the rim of the cup in a nervous gesture Esther had not seen before today.

"I wasn't much good to the army with only one foot, so they sent me home. Despite the pain, I was glad. You see, all the time I was traveling, I pictured a joyful reunion with Diana. Instead, she stared at me, horrified. Three days after I returned, she gave me back my ring, telling me she wanted to marry a farmer and that I couldn't be a good farmer with only one foot."

Esther gasped, horrified by the evidence that Diana's love had been so shallow and by the realization that although more than two decades had passed, Jeremy was still suffering from Diana's rejection.

"I can't believe anyone would be so cruel." Though she'd known Jeremy less than two weeks, Esther knew he was a good, honorable man, the kind of man who made dreams come true. But Diana had thrown his love away.

"The war destroyed so many dreams," she said softly.

∞

Jeremy stared at Esther, more touched than he had thought possible by the sheen of tears in her eyes. She'd cared—really cared—about what had happened between him and Diana all those years ago. And now, if he read her correctly, she was opening the door to her past.

"Is that what happened to you? Your dreams were destroyed?"

She nodded. "We weren't officially betrothed, but Chester and I had an unspoken agreement that we'd marry when the war was over." A bittersweet smile crossed her face as she said, "I'd known him my whole life."

As her eyes darkened at the memory, Jeremy felt a twinge of jealousy at the evidence of a love far stronger than what he and Diana had shared. Esther and Chester had been fortunate.

"Everyone joked that we were meant to be together because our names were so similar," Esther continued. "We thought we were invincible, but we weren't. Chester was killed in the first day of fighting at Gettysburg."

"And you've never married."

"No."

"Why not?" Jeremy couldn't imagine that she'd lacked for suitors, especially here where men far outnumbered women.

Esther's eyes were somber. "No one else could compare."

It was what he'd feared.

Chapter 6

"You look happy, Mr. Snyder." Jeremy's landlady wiped her hands on a towel as he entered the kitchen looking for a cup of coffee to keep him awake while he painted.

"I am happy," he admitted, though he was surprised it was obvious. "I'm beginning to think I might settle down in Cheyenne."

Though he had felt a moment of despair when he'd heard the story of Chester, the last few days had given him hope that there might be a future for him here and that Esther might be part of that future.

Mrs. Tyson nodded, her eyes narrowing as she studied him. "It's a good place to live. When Abel went to heaven, my sister wanted me to move back to Illinois. I was tempted for a day or two, but then I realized that Cheyenne's my home."

Like Esther. The difference was, Esther had never had a husband. Jeremy felt his heart clench at all that she had missed. Anyone could see that she would have been a wonderful wife and mother. All you had to do was look at how she'd raised Susan and the way she treated her customers to know that she had an abundance of love to share. And then there was the way she'd dealt with him, paying him more than he'd asked, serving him dinner each day, helping him find new clients. That was wonderful, but there was more. Jeremy sighed softly, remembering the glances Esther had given him, the sparkle in her eyes, the sweet smile that accompanied those looks. It was enough to make a man dream. And so he had.

"I guess you'll be looking for a permanent place to live once you marry." Mrs. Tyson's words brought him back to the present. "I'll miss you," she said, "but it's plain as the nose on my face that you've changed in the last few weeks. You're wearing the look of a man in love."

Jeremy hadn't realized it was so obvious. It was true that he'd never felt like this, not even with Diana. Everything seemed different. Colors were brighter, sounds sweeter, even his painting was better. When he sat by the easel, he felt as if his ideas were being translated into images almost without conscious effort. He'd completed two new landscapes in less time than ever before, but the quality had not suffered. To the contrary, this was the best work he'd ever done.

He smiled as he pushed open the door to his

room and set the carafe of coffee on the bureau. If this was what love brought, he never wanted it to end. And maybe, just maybe, it wouldn't have to.

Opening one of the drawers, he pulled out his money sack and counted the contents. It would be a stretch, but this was something he wanted to do.

"He's courting you."

"Nonsense!" The idea was appealing—very appealing, but Esther knew better than to assign too much importance to the invitation. "He simply wants to thank me for all the meals I've cooked."

Susan shook her head and returned to brushing Esther's hair. Though Esther had protested the extra effort, saying she could wear her normal hairstyle, Susan had been adamant that a special evening demanded a special coiffure and a special dress.

"That might be what he said, but I have eyes." Susan shook her head again. "I've seen the way he looks at you, and it's not like you're a cook. Besides, if all he wanted to do was thank you, he wouldn't have invited you to the InterOcean. There are plenty of other restaurants in Cheyenne, but he chose the most exclusive one."

"I know." And that had bothered Esther. Though she'd never eaten there, she knew that the hotel's dining room was renowned for both its fine cuisine and its high prices. "I told Jeremy it was too expensive, but he insisted."

Susan wrapped a lock of Esther's hair around the curling iron. "It's what I told you. He's courting you, and only the best will do." She released the curl and studied the way it framed Esther's face. "Perfect. Jeremy will like this."

When he arrived an hour later, it appeared that Susan had been correct, for Jeremy was speechless for a second. Clearing his throat, he said, "You look beautiful, Esther."

As color flooded her cheeks, Esther tried to control her reaction. It had been many years since she'd dressed to please a man, and she hadn't been certain she would succeed. The fact that Jeremy's eyes gleamed with admiration set her heart to pounding.

"It's the dress," she said, running her hands over the purple silk. "I had it made for the wedding, but Susan insisted I wear it tonight." The gown had been beautiful when Mrs. Bradford had finished it, but unbeknownst to Esther, Susan had spent countless hours embroidering a row of lilacs around the hem. The delicate flowers captured in floss had turned a beautiful gown into one that was truly spectacular.

Jeremy shook his head. "Your beauty is more

than the dress. I'll be the envy of every man at the hotel." He reached for Esther's heavy woolen cloak and settled it over her shoulders. "And now, if you're ready. . ." He bent his arm and placed Esther's hand on it. "I hope you don't mind walking."

Esther did not. Though Jeremy had proposed hiring a carriage, she had insisted that she was capable of walking the one block to the InterOcean. Her initial thought had been to save him the expense, but now that they were on their way, she realized how much she enjoyed walking at Jeremy's side, having her hand nestled on his arm, feeling as if she was part of a couple. This was the stuff of dreams. And when they entered the hotel and were ushered to the dining room, the pleasure only increased.

"This is even more beautiful than I'd expected," Esther said when they were seated. With its polished dark wainscoting and coffered ceiling, the dining room exuded elegance, while the white table linens and shiny wallpaper brightened what could have been a dark room.

"You mean you've never been here?"

She shook her head. There were so many things she'd never done, and dining with a handsome man was one of them. "A woman alone doesn't eat in places like this. It would have been awkward." There were no tables for one.

"Then I'm doubly glad we came." Jeremy smiled, and the warmth in his expression made Esther's pulse begin to race. Was Susan right? Could Jeremy be courting her? Was it possible that her dreams of marriage and happily-ever-after might come true?

"I feel honored to be the one who introduced you to this restaurant." Though his words were matter-of-fact, Jeremy's tone caused her heart to skip a beat. Truly, this was the most wonderful evening imaginable.

When the food arrived, Jeremy bowed his head and offered thanks for the meal, then waited until Esther had tasted her trout before he picked up his fork.

"The food is delicious," she said, savoring the delicate sauce. Perfectly prepared food shared with the perfect companion. She could ask for nothing more.

Jeremy cut a piece of his meat and chewed slowly before he said, "It's not as good as yours."

Esther did not believe that. "There's no need for flattery."

"It's not flattery. It's the truth. The stew you served on Wednesday was more flavorful than this bison."

It couldn't be true, but Esther appreciated the

thought, just as she appreciated everything Jeremy was doing to make tonight so special. "I enjoy cooking," she told him, "and I'm more than happy to share it with you." It felt so good—so right—having Jeremy at her kitchen table. His presence there made her heart pound and fueled her dreams.

He nodded, as if he'd heard her unspoken words, and Esther blushed. "Your cooking is superb," Jeremy said, "but the company is even better. I've enjoyed these past few weeks more than any I can recall."

And then the bubble of happiness burst. Though his words touched her heart, Esther heard the finality in them. Tonight wasn't simply a thank you. It was an early good-bye. Jeremy was reminding her that he would soon be leaving Cheyenne.

Mustering every bit of strength she possessed, Esther smiled. "I'm the one who's grateful. If it weren't for you, my dream of giving Susan her Christmas star would have remained just that—a dream. Thanks to you, she will have something she can treasure for the rest of her life."

And Esther would have memories of these few sweet weeks when Jeremy was part of her life. He filled the empty spaces deep inside her. He made ordinary days special. He brought color to what had been a gray life. Esther lowered her eyes and pretended that the trout demanded her attention. She didn't want Jeremy to read the emotion in her eyes.

Just being in the same room with him lifted her spirits, and when he smiled at her, Esther's heart overflowed with happiness. She placed a piece of trout on her fork and raised it to her lips. She could deny it no longer. She loved Jeremy. He was the man who'd put a spring in her step. He was kind, talented, and generous. Oh, why mince words? Jeremy was everything she'd dreamed of in a man. If only they had a future.

But they did not. He was leaving, and she was staying. That was the way it had to be. Even if Jeremy had asked her to go with him, Esther would have refused. If there was one thing she knew, it was that she would be miserable sharing the itinerant life that was so important to him. And misery was the quickest way to destroy love. Esther wouldn't take that risk, for it wasn't only her heart that was at stake. Jeremy had been hurt once. She would not be the one to hurt him a second time.

Chapter 7

"I don't understand it." Jeremy muttered the words under his breath as he sat on the edge of the chair and unstrapped his left foot. He'd believed Esther would be pleased by dinner at the InterOcean, and for a while it had seemed that she was enjoying not just the food and atmosphere but also his company. Her eyes had shone with what he thought was genuine happiness, and her cheeks had borne a most becoming flush. Then suddenly the lovely glow had faded, and only a blind man would have missed the sadness in her eyes. Esther had said all the right words, but Jeremy could tell that she wasn't happy and that had spoiled the evening for him.

He wanted Esther to be happy. Oh, how he wanted her to be happy. But she wasn't, and he wasn't certain why. Though he'd replayed the evening a dozen times, trying to understand what had caused the change, the only clue he had was that she'd looked sorrowful when she spoke of the Christmas star. Perhaps Esther's thoughts had returned to the past, and she'd wished she'd had her own star, that Chester had survived the war and given her the life she'd dreamed of.

Jeremy rubbed petroleum jelly into his stump as he did each night. Though that eased the pain in his leg, it did nothing to assuage the pain in his heart. He hadn't been lying when he told Esther that he enjoyed seeing new parts of the country. What he hadn't told her was that the itinerant life was lonely. For years, Jeremy had prayed for a home of his own and a woman to share it. And now when it seemed that his prayers were close to being answered, he feared that once again they'd be dashed, unless he could find a way to make Esther happy. Jeremy couldn't bring Chester back to life, but surely there was something he could do to make her eyes sparkle again.

All he had to do was find it.

⁓∞⁓

What a fool she was! Esther winced as the brush tangled in her hair, but that pain was nothing compared to the pain in her heart. She had spoiled a perfectly wonderful evening by worrying about her future. Hadn't she learned anything in her thirty-eight years? She knew she couldn't control the future. Only God could. She knew she needed to trust Him. He'd healed her heart after Chester's death; He'd brought her here and shown her the way to succeed. He would guide her to her future, if only she would let Him.

Her hair needed to be braided, but that could wait. There was a greater need right now. Esther reached for the Bible on her bedside table and opened it to the book of Jeremiah. Chapter 29, verse 11 had always brought her comfort, and it did not fail her now: "For I know the thoughts that I think toward you, saith the Lord, thoughts of peace, and not of evil, to give you an expected end."

Esther closed her eyes, letting the words sink into her heart. When she felt the familiar comfort settle over her, she read the next verse. "Then shall ye call upon me, and ye shall go and pray unto me, and I will hearken unto you." The promise of peace was there, but if she wanted it, she needed to ask for it. Kneeling beside her bed, Esther bowed her head. "Dear Lord, help me find joy in each day. Show me the path You have prepared for me."

Though the future was still clouded, that night she slept better than she had in months.

❧

From her vantage point behind the counter, Esther watched as Jeremy put the final brushstroke on the painting.

"We're finished, Susan."

"Can I see it?" Susan asked as she slid from the stool. "You've been so secretive."

Jeremy shook his head. "Your aunt told me that's part of the tradition. Although others can see the portrait, you need to wait until your wedding day."

Susan's pout drew Esther to her niece's side, and if that meant that she was near to Jeremy, that was all right, too. Though she'd tried her best to regain the special feeling of closeness they'd shared at the InterOcean, Esther had failed. It seemed as though a barrier had been erected between them, and nothing she said or did demolished it. Jeremy seemed preoccupied. He'd even stopped eating with her and Susan, claiming he had work to do and couldn't afford the time. The worst part was that although Esther suspected she had created the barrier, she had no idea how to make it disappear.

"Jeremy's right. It's only eight more days." A quick glance at the canvas confirmed what Esther had thought: the painting was magnificent. Turning to Jeremy, she raised an eyebrow. "When will you have it framed?"

"Two days. It needs to be completely dry first. If it's convenient for you, I'll bring it Saturday afternoon on my way back from Mrs. Edgar's house."

This was what Esther had feared. Today would

be the end of her time with Jeremy. Oh, she'd see him occasionally while he was still in Cheyenne, but those wonderful days of sharing meals and conversations with him, of having only to look across the room to see him were over.

"The offer of using the bakery as your studio is still open," she said, hoping she didn't sound as if she were pleading.

He nodded as he dipped his brush into turpentine. "I appreciate that, but Mrs. Edgar doesn't want anyone to know she's having her portrait painted. Apparently her husband has been asking for a miniature to put in his watch for years. When Mrs. Edgar heard about Susan and Michael's portrait, she decided this would be the year Mr. Edgar got his wish."

"Will you have enough time to finish it?" Susan's portrait had taken almost three weeks to complete.

Jeremy nodded again. "I just won't be sleeping very much." Or sharing meals with her.

"I'm sure it'll be as wonderful as Susan's portrait." Esther darted another glance at the finished work. Jeremy had captured more than Susan and Michael's features; he'd captured their love. Though the other Christmas stars were beautiful, this one was spectacular. "I can never thank you enough."

"It was truly my pleasure." For the first time since the night at the InterOcean, Jeremy's smile seemed unfettered. As the clock chimed, the smile turned into a frown. "I'm sorry to rush away, but I have another appointment this afternoon."

A minute later he was gone, leaving Esther with an enormous void deep inside her.

∞

Jeremy pulled his watch from his pocket, trying not to scowl when he realized that the store would close in five minutes. If he were able, he'd run, but running had not been a possibility since Antietam. When he opened the door to Mullen's Fine Jewelry, the clock was striking five, and the proprietor seemed on the verge of locking the door.

"Thank you for waiting for me. I'm sorry I'm so late." Jeremy brushed snow from his coat. "Were you able to find one?"

As the jeweler shook his head, his elaborately waxed and curled moustache wiggled. "I sent telegrams to my best suppliers, but no one had what you want."

Though he'd feared this would be the case, Jeremy could not disguise his disappointment. "I know I didn't give you much notice."

Mr. Mullen stepped behind the main display

case. The assortment of gold and silver pieces, many decorated with gemstones or pearls, was the best in Cheyenne, yet it held no appeal for Jeremy. There was only one thing he wanted.

"That's true," Mr. Mullen agreed. "You didn't give me much notice. On top of that, it's a busy time of the year for every jeweler. I was afraid I would not be able to find it. That's why—"

Jeremy had heard enough. This was one dream that would not come true. "There's no need to apologize, Mr. Mullen. I know you did your best. The fault is mine."

The jeweler fingered his moustache, almost as if he was trying to hide a smile. That was absurd. There was no reason to smile.

"If you'd let me finish, you'd know that I wasn't going to apologize." Mr. Mullen's words came out as little more than a reprimand. "When you first approached me, I knew it was unlikely anyone would have what you need. That's why I took the liberty of making one." He reached under the counter and brought out a cloth bag. "Is this what you had in mind?"

Jeremy stared in amazement at the object in Mr. Mullen's hand. It was everything he'd dreamed of and more. "It's perfect."

∞

"Is something wrong, Aunt Esther?"

Startled by her niece's approach, Esther dropped the rolling pin. As she bent down to retrieve it, she frowned when she saw the amount of flour she'd spilled onto the floor. This wasn't like her. But then the way she'd been feeling for the past few days wasn't like her, either. Despite her prayers, the future was still unclear.

"Nothing's wrong." Though Esther had hoped that her indecision hadn't been obvious, Susan had seen behind the mask she'd been wearing. "I'm simply extra busy this year." That wasn't a lie, but it also wasn't the whole truth. Esther had spent far too much time dreaming about a future that would never happen.

Susan perched on the edge of a chair. "It's my wedding, isn't it? I should never have planned a Christmas wedding. I know how busy the bakery is during December."

After rinsing the rolling pin, Esther resumed her work on the pie crusts, grateful that the task kept her back to Susan. She didn't want her niece to see the confusion she knew was reflected in her eyes. "It's not your fault, Susan. This is the perfect time for you and Michael to marry. I wouldn't have it any other way." Being busy should have kept her mind focused on happier thoughts than Jeremy's absence.

"But something is wrong," Susan persisted. "I can tell."

Esther hadn't planned to say anything to Susan until she'd made her decision, but the girl's obvious concern made her admit, "I've been thinking about my future. I'm trying to decide whether I should sell the bakery."

"What?" Susan jumped up from the chair and put her arm around Esther's waist, turning her until they were facing. "You said this was your home. Your life."

Esther nodded slowly. "That's true. You and the bakery have been my life for the last ten years." She laid a finger under Susan's chin, tipping it upward. "They've been wonderful years, but it feels as if they've been a season in my life and now that season is ending."

Susan was silent for a moment, her eyes searching Esther's face as if she sought a meaning behind the words. "If you do sell the bakery, you can live with Michael and me."

Her niece's generous offer did not surprise Esther, but there was only one possible answer. "Thank you, Susan, but I cannot do that. You and Michael are starting your life together. As much as I love you, I know it would be wrong for me to be part of that life."

Susan looked bewildered. "But what would you do?"

"I'm not sure." That was the reason Esther hadn't slept last night. "I know what I want to do, but I'm not sure that's possible." If wishes came true and prayers were answered, she would spend the rest of her life with Jeremy, but he'd never spoken of love or of wanting her to be a permanent part of his life.

Bewilderment turned to a calculating look as Susan stared at her, and for the briefest of moments Esther feared her niece had read her thoughts. Impossible.

"Aren't you the one who told me Grandma Hathaway said Christmas was the season of miracles?"

Esther nodded, remembering the number of times her mother had said exactly that. "Yes, but..."

"Then start praying for one."

Esther did.

Chapter 8

Three days until Christmas. Jeremy peered into the mirror as he wielded his razor. No point in nicking sensitive skin. They'd be a busy three days, but he wasn't complaining. No, sirree. If everything went the way he prayed it would, if he had enough courage to do all that he planned, this would be his best Christmas ever.

The first part was easy. He would finish Mrs. Edgar's portrait this afternoon, frame it tomorrow night and then deliver it early on Christmas Eve morning. The second part was more difficult. Laying down the razor, he studied his face. No whiskers visible. He rinsed the bits of shaving cream from his face, then toweled it dry. Those were all mechanical tasks, things he did every day. What he was contemplating was far more difficult.

He'd completed the other painting last night so that it, too, would be ready for delivery on Christmas Eve or perhaps Christmas morning. The question was whether he could muster the courage to do that. While it had seemed like a good idea when he'd first considered it, now he wasn't so certain. But there was no need to make a decision this morning. He had three more days.

Dressing quickly, he descended the stairs for breakfast. First things first. He'd put the final touches on Mrs. Edgar's portrait, then think about the other one.

"You have a letter, Mr. Snyder." Mrs. Tyson grinned as she handed him a cream-colored envelope. "A young woman just delivered it."

Jeremy hadn't been expecting mail, and he didn't recognize the handwriting. Carefully running his finger beneath the flap, he opened the envelope and withdrew the heavy card, his eyes widening in surprise when he realized it was an invitation to Susan's wedding. Why had she invited him? Susan had said it was going to be a fairly small wedding, with only her and Michael's family and a few close friends. Jeremy didn't fit into either category.

Uncertain how to reply, he slid the card back into the envelope, then realized there was a second piece of paper inside it. That was ordinary stationery, not the heavier vellum of the invitation. Curious, he unfolded the sheet and read:

Dear Mr. Snyder,
    I hope you will join us on Christmas Eve. We attend services at 11:00 p.m. Afterward, Michael's parents have invited us all for supper at their hotel. I know this is short notice, but it would bring me much pleasure to have you as part of our group. You need not reply, but if you can come, please arrive at our home at 10:30 p.m.
                   Sincerely yours,
                   Susan Mitchell

Jeremy sank onto the hallway bench, trying to regain his equilibrium in the face of this extraordinary missive. By rights, the invitation should have come from Esther, not Susan. By rights, Jeremy should refuse it. Yet what if this was the answer he sought, the impetus he needed to gather his courage?

Jeremy nodded. When he'd read Susan's note, he'd envisioned himself walking to church with Esther at his side, sitting next to her, sharing a hymnal with her, and afterward. . .

This was one invitation he would not refuse.

                       ⚬∞⚬

"Now, aren't you glad I convinced you to wear this gown?" As Susan slid the last button into its loop, she turned Esther toward the cheval glass. "Look."

Esther stared at her reflection in the mirror, not quite believing what she saw. The burgundy silk with the elaborate bustle and the double box pleats circling the hem was the most elegant garment she had ever owned, and the intricate hairstyle Susan had insisted complemented the gown left Esther feeling as if she were looking at a stranger. An elegant stranger.

"Are you sure this is me?"

Susan nodded. "The new you. You want to make a good impression on Michael's parents, don't you?" Though Esther had had more than a few minutes' worry over her first meeting with the elder Porters, Susan's almost secretive smile made her think her niece had something else in mind. That was silly, of course, for what else could Susan be thinking of?

"It's very kind of Michael's parents to host supper tonight." The couple had arrived in town only this morning but had made all the arrangements in advance, telling Esther they wanted to thank her for the many meals she had given Michael over the course of his courtship.

It was the same argument Jeremy had made when he'd invited her to dine at the InterOcean, but tonight would be far different from that evening. Though Esther had no doubt that the meal would be enjoyable, she was not filled with the same anticipation she'd felt before. The reason was simple: instead of being half of a couple, tonight Esther would be part of a group, a group that did not include Jeremy.

A firm knock on the door broke her reverie. "The Porters are early," she said, glancing at the clock on the bureau.

"Do you mind going?" Susan gestured toward the lock of hair that had somehow come loose from her coiffure.

Knowing her niece wanted everything to be perfect, Esther headed toward the door. When she opened it, she stared in amazement as the blood drained from her face.

"Jeremy! Is something wrong?"

❧

His heart sank. This was not the reception he'd expected. Though he'd suspected that Susan had sent the invitation without consulting Esther, he had assumed she would have told her before now. The shock on Esther's face made it clear that she had not expected him.

"As far as I know, nothing's wrong," Jeremy said, trying not to stare at the woman who held his heart in her hands. "Susan invited me to join you tonight. I thought you knew."

Though she was clearly flustered, Esther looked more than usually pretty tonight. It might be the fancy dress or those loose curls that danced against her cheeks. It could simply be the flush that colored her face. Jeremy didn't care about the reason. All he cared about was whether or not this beautiful woman would allow him to share Christmas Eve with her.

"Come in," she said, ushering him into the sitting room. "We'll be ready to leave in a few minutes."

Though the words were ordinary, Esther's voice sounded strained. It could be nothing more than the shock of an unexpected guest, but Jeremy feared the reason was more serious. Perhaps he'd misread her earlier friendliness. Perhaps it had been nothing more than charity that had made her be so kind. Perhaps she saw him only as the man who'd painted Susan's portrait. All of that was possible, but Jeremy refused to believe it. He wouldn't give up so easily.

"I can see that my coming is a surprise. I should have considered that, but to be honest, since the day I received Susan's invitation, all I've thought about was being with you again."

Esther's eyes darkened, and her lips turned up in a sweet smile. Before she could speak, Jeremy continued. "If you'd rather I leave. . ." He had to make the offer, though he hoped against hope that she would refuse.

"No, of course not." The color in her cheeks deepened. "I'm so happy to see you again." Though Esther started to say something more, Susan rushed into the room, her brown eyes twinkling with what appeared to be mischief. "Aunt Esther and I are glad you're here."

"Yes we are." The warmth in Esther's expression sent a rush of pleasure through Jeremy's veins. It appeared that coming here tonight had not been a mistake.

∽

Perhaps it was a mistake, but if it was, Esther would have all her tomorrows to regret it. No matter what the morning brought, she intended to enjoy the simple pleasure of being with Jeremy tonight. Perhaps she should have chided Susan for issuing such an inappropriate invitation and neglecting to tell her about it, but Esther could not, not when that invitation had brought her what she longed for: time with Jeremy.

There was no time for private conversation, for the once-quiet sitting room felt as crowded and noisy as the train depot when Michael and his parents arrived.

Though the Porters appeared to be as charming as their son, Esther barely heard a word they said. Instead, her gaze kept meeting Jeremy's, and she found herself wishing they were alone. The opportunity came sooner than she had thought possible.

"Esther and I can walk," Jeremy said when Mr. Porter explained that he had hired a carriage but that it might be a bit crowded with six passengers. "If she agrees."

Esther did. Minutes later they were walking down Sixteenth Street. It felt like the night they'd dined at the InterOcean as they strolled along the street with Esther's hand nestled in the crook of Jeremy's arm. But tonight would be different. Esther was determined to do nothing to spoil the evening. Tonight was a night to celebrate the wonder of God's love and the greatest gift the world had ever received. Sharing that joyous message and the hope that accompanied it with Jeremy only made the night more special.

As happened each year, the church was crowded, the scents of perfume and Macassar oil mingled with the pungent odors of candle wax and wet wool. Yet no one seemed to mind the crowding or the smells, least of all Esther. Even if it was only for a few hours, she was with Jeremy.

When the first hymn began, she discovered that his voice was as off-key as her own, but that didn't matter. What mattered was that they were worshiping together. Judging from the expression on his face, Jeremy was as moved as she by the minister's reading from the Gospel of Luke.

" 'Fear not: for behold I bring you good tidings of great joy, which shall be to all people.' "

Esther felt the prickle of tears in her eyes as joy filled her heart. Even if her prayer for a miracle was not answered, this was a Christmas she would never forget.

"Are you certain you want to walk again?" Mr. Porter asked when the service had ended and they'd filed outside. "We could let the young people do that."

Jeremy turned toward Esther. "If Esther's willing, I'd prefer to walk. It's a beautiful night."

It was indeed. The wind had subsided, leaving a star-studded sky with a few lazy snowflakes drifting to the ground.

"I'd like to walk." And to share more of this night with the man who had captured her heart.

They strolled in silence for a few minutes. When they were two blocks from the church and the crowd had dispersed, Jeremy stopped.

"The beautiful night wasn't the only reason I wanted to walk." He reached into his greatcoat pocket and withdrew a cloth bag. "I have a gift for you." His voice sounded almost hesitant, as if he were afraid of her reaction.

Esther stared at the dark green velvet sack, her heart leaping at the thought that this wonderful man had brought her a gift. "I didn't expect anything." Just being here with Jeremy was more than she had expected.

"I know you didn't, but I want you to have this." He placed the bag in her hand.

As her fingers reached inside and touched the familiar shape, Esther gasped. It couldn't be, yet it was. Gently she pulled out the star-shaped frame. Similar in size to the one she'd bought for Susan's portrait, this frame was more ornate, with open filigree decorating each of the points. And in the center. . . Esther took a deep breath, hardly able to believe her eyes. All her life she had longed for her own Christmas star, and now Jeremy had given it to her. Looking back at her from one side of the painting was her portrait. The other side was nothing more than blank canvas.

"It's beautiful, Jeremy, but I don't understand. I didn't pose for this." What Esther really didn't understand was what he meant by the gift. He knew the tradition.

He gave her a smile so sweet it brought tears to her eyes. "You didn't need to pose. Your image is engraved on my heart. All I had to do was close my eyes, and I pictured you."

Esther nodded. Though she was not an artist, she had no trouble picturing Jeremy when they were apart.

His expression sobered. "I wanted to give you a finished star, but I couldn't, because I wasn't certain what you wanted on the other side." He paused for a second. "I can paint a landscape there. That may not be like the others, but it's important to me that you have your own star. I know you've dreamed of one, and I want to make your dreams come true."

Esther looked at the star, marveling at the way Jeremy had portrayed her. It was her face, yet it wasn't. She had never seen herself looking so beautiful, so in love. Was this how Jeremy saw her?

He took a shallow breath before he continued. "I know how I want to finish the portrait. In my dreams, it's my face next to yours." Jeremy's voice rang with emotion. "More than anything, I want to be part of your Christmas star and part of your life."

Esther stared at the man she loved so dearly, the man whose words were making her heart pound with excitement. He said he wanted to make her dreams come true, and he was doing exactly that. When she opened her mouth to speak, he raised a cautioning hand.

"I know I can't take Chester's place, but I want whatever place in your life you can give me." Jeremy paused for a second and took her left hand in his. "I love you with all my heart. Will you marry me?"

Her heart overflowing with love, Esther nodded. Susan had been right. All she needed to do was ask God for a miracle, and He'd granted it. "Oh, Jeremy, there is nothing I want more than to marry you. It's true that I loved Chester and that he'll always have a place in my heart, but my love for you is stronger than anything I've ever known." The words came tumbling out like water over a falls as Esther tried to express the depth of her love.

She squeezed Jeremy's hand, wishing the cold night hadn't dictated gloves. "I think I fell in love with you that first day when you walked into the bakery. I had never felt that kind of instant connection before, but it was there, and it's only grown stronger since then. Marrying you will make my life complete."

"And mine." Jeremy's eyes shone with happiness that rivaled the stars' brilliance. "Oh, my love, you've made me happier than I dreamed possible."

When Esther smiled, he drew her into his arms

and pressed his lips to hers, giving her the sweetest of kisses. His lips were warm and tender, his caress more wonderful than even her wildest dreams, and in that moment Esther knew this was where she belonged: in Jeremy's arms.

When at length they broke apart, she smiled at the man she loved, the man who was going to be her husband. "It may take a while, but I'll sell the bakery so we can travel wherever you want."

His eyes widened, and she saw him swallow, as if trying to control his emotions. "You'd do that for me?" Jeremy's voice cracked as he pronounced the words.

Nodding, Esther explained. "A month ago, I felt as if the bakery and Cheyenne were my home. Then I met you, and I learned that home is more than a building or even a city. Home is the place you share with the person you love."

Jeremy matched her nod. "Will you share your home with me?" Esther's confusion must have shown, for he continued. "I've learned a few things, too. One is that I want to stay here. Cheyenne will be my home as long as I'm with the woman I love."

"Oh, Jeremy!" Esther raised her lips for another kiss as snowflakes drifted past them. "You've made all my dreams come true."

"And so have you, my Christmas star bride."

About the Author

Amanda Cabot is the author of more than thirty novels, including the CBA bestseller *Christmas Roses* and *Waiting for Spring*, which is also set in Cheyenne. A Christmastime bride herself, Amanda now lives in Cheyenne with her high-school sweetheart husband. You can find her at www.amandacabot.com

The Advent Bride
by Mary Connealy

Dedication

This book is dedicated to Steven Curtis Chapman, who sang a really encouraging song, "Love Take Me Over," at a time I really needed encouragement. Thank you to all the wonderful, blessed artists in contemporary Christian music.

Chapter 1

Lone Tree, Nebraska
Monday, November 29, 1875

Being a teacher was turning out to be a little like having the flu.

Simon O'Keeffe. Her heart broke for him at the same time her stomach twisted with dread for herself. The churning innards this boy caused in her made a case of influenza fun and games.

The small form on the front steps of the Lone Tree schoolhouse huddled against the cold. Shivering herself, she wondered how long seven-year-old Simon had been sitting with his back pressed against the building to get out of the wind.

On these smooth, treeless highlands the wind blew nearly all the time. No matter where a person sought shelter outside, there was no escape from the Nebraska cold.

Just as there was no escape from Simon.

Picking up her pace and shoving her dread down

deep, she hurried to the door, produced the key her position as school marm had granted her, and said, "Let's get inside, Simon. You must be freezing."

And what was his worthless father thinking to let him get to school so early?

Simon's eyes, sullen and far too smart, lifted to hers.

"Did you walk to school?" Melanie tried to sound pleasant. But it didn't matter. Simon would take it wrong. The cantankerous little guy had a gift for it. She swung the door open and waved her hand to shoo him in.

The spark of rebellion in his eyes clashed with his trembling. He wanted to defy her—Simon always wanted to defy her—but he was just too cold.

"My pa ain't gonna leave me to walk to school in this cold, Miss Douglas." Simon was offended on his father's behalf.

"So he drove you in?" Melanie should just quit talking. Nothing she said would make Simon respond well, the poor little holy terror.

"We live in town now. . .leastways we're living here for the winter."

And that explained Simon's presence. He'd started the school year, then he'd stayed home to help with harvest—or maybe his pa had just been too busy to get the boy out the door. And before harvest was over, the weather turned bitter cold. The five-mile walk was too hard, and apparently his pa wouldn't drive him.

The day Simon had stopped coming to school, her life as the teacher had improved dramatically. That didn't mean the rest of her life wasn't miserable, but at least school had been good. And now here came her little arch enemy back to school. It was all she could do to suppress a groan.

Closing the door, Melanie rushed to set her books on her desk in the frigid room. She headed straight for the pot-bellied stove to get a fire going.

Gathering an armful of logs, she pulled open the creaking door and knelt to stuff kindling into the stove. She added shredded bits of bark and touched a match to it. A crash startled her. She knocked her head into the cast iron.

Whirling around, expecting the worst. . .she got it.

Simon.

Glaring at her.

Around his scruffy boots lay a pile of books that had previously sat in a tidy pile on her desk.

Dear God, I'm already weary, and it's just gone seven in the morning, with nearly two hours until the other children show up. She was on her knees. What better to do than pray?

The prayer helped her fight back her temper. After seeing no harm was done—not counting the new bump on her forehead—she turned and went back to stoking the fire.

Melanie swung the little iron door shut and twisted the flat knob that kept the fire inside. "Come on over and get warm, Simon." Kneeling by the slowly warming stove put heart into her. Her room at Mrs. Rathbone's was miserable. She spent every night in a mostly unheated attic.

Simon came close, he must have been freezing to move next to her.

The little boy's dark curls were too long. He was dressed in near rags. Was his father poor? Maybe a widower didn't notice worn-out knees and threadbare cuffs. And it didn't cost a thing to get a haircut, not if Henry O'Keeffe did the cutting himself. Water was certainly free, but the boy had black curves under his ragged fingernails and dirt on his neck.

Pieces of cooked egg stuck on the front of Simon's shirt, too. Sloppy as that was, it gave Melanie some encouragement to know the boy had been served a hot breakfast.

The crackling fire was heartening, and the boy was close enough to get warm. She reached out her hands to garner those first precious waves of heat.

"Soon, I'll have to get to work, Simon. But you can stay here, just sit by the stove and keep warm."

A scowl twisted his face. What had she said now?

"It ain't my pa's doing that I was out there. He told me to go to school at school time. I'm the one that got the time wrong."

Leave a seven-year-old to get himself to school. Henry O'Keeffe had a lot to answer for.

"Well, I hope you weren't waiting long. I'm usually here by seven, so you can come on over early if you want." The twisting stomach came back. She didn't want this little imp here from early morning on.

But she'd just invited the most unruly little boy in town to share her peaceful time at the school. Just the thought of dealing with him for more hours that absolutely necessary reminded Melanie of influenza again. Her stomach twisted with dismay.

But what could be done? The boy couldn't sit out in the cold.

God had no words of wisdom for her except the plain truth. She was stuck with Simon O'Keeffe. She'd have to make the best of it and help the boy any way she could.

Chapter 2

"Class dismissed." Melanie clasped the *McGuffey Reader* in both hands and did her best to keep her face serene while she strangled the book. It had to be better than strangling a seven-year-old.

Every child in the place erupted from their seats and ran for the nails where their coats hung.

"Simon." Melanie's voice cut through the clatter. Simon stood, belligerent. He held his desktop in his hands.

The three boys older than Simon laughed and shoved each other. There had been none of this roughhousing last week. They'd been acting up all day, reacting to Simon's bold defiance. She'd lost all control of the older boys. Four older girls giggled. Two little boys just a year older than Simon slid looks of pity his way. They all scrambled for their coats and lunch pails.

It hadn't helped that she'd started practice today for a Christmas program, scheduled for Christmas Eve, here at the school. Melanie had been warned that the entire town, not just parents, would be attending.

"Yes, Miss Douglas?"

Do not render evil for evil.

Why that was right there in the Bible. Was disassembling a desk evil? Normally Melanie would have said no, but this was Simon.

"You will stay after school until you've put that desk back together." Melanie hadn't even known the desks could be taken apart. They'd always seemed very sturdy to her. But she'd underestimated her little foe.

"I can finish it tomorrow. Pa will worry about me." Simon stood, holding that desktop, the little rat trying to wriggle his way out of this trap. The boy was apparently bored to death with school. Studying would've made the day go faster, but that was too much to ask.

"When you don't arrive home on time, he'll come hunting for you, and this is the first place he'll check."

"But he said he might be late."

"How late?" Melanie clamped her mouth shut.

Simon's eyes blazed. The boy was always ready to take offense on his father's behalf.

Melanie had to stop saying a single word Simon could take as a criticism of his pa and address her concerns directly to Henry. But she wasn't letting Simon leave for a possibly cold house with no father at home. Simon's after-school time was, as of this moment, lasting until his pa turned up to fetch him.

"Get on with repairing the desk. Then you can bring your books close to the stove, and we'll study until you've made up for the schooltime you wasted taking your desk apart."

Simon glared at her, but he turned back to the desk. Melanie opened her book to study for tomorrow's lesson. The two of them got along very well, as long as the whole room was between them and neither spoke.

"It's done. Can I go now?"

Melanie lifted her head. She'd gotten lost in her reading. One of the older children, Lisa Manchon, was in an advanced arithmetic book. The girl was restless, ready to be done with school and, at fifteen years old, find a husband and get on with a life of her own.

Her folks, though, wouldn't hear of such a thing, or perhaps there were no offers. For whatever reason, Lisa was kept in school. Melanie worked hard to keep her interested in her work.

"No, you *may* not go." Melanie stressed the correct grammar. "Bring your reader to the stove, and we'll go over tomorrow's lesson together."

November days were short in Nebraska, and the

sun was low in the sky. Obviously Henry was not yet home or he'd have come to find his son. Melanie carried her heavy desk chair to the stove and stood, brows arched, waiting for Simon to come join her.

It helped that it was cold.

As they worked, Simon proved, as he always did when he bothered to try, that he was one of the brightest children in the school.

The school door slammed open.

"Simon is missing!" In charged a tall man wrapped up in a thick coat with a scarf and Stetson, gloves and heavy boots.

Henry O'Keeffe—here at last.

He skidded to a halt. His light blue eyes flashed like cold fire—at her. Then he looked more warmly at his son. "Simon, I told you to go home after school."

"Pa, she wouldn't—" The little tattletale.

"Your son," Melanie cut through their talk, "had to stay after school for misbehaving, Mr. O'Keeffe." Unlike her unruly young student, she had no trouble taking full responsibility for her actions.

She rose from her chair by the fire. "Is it a long way home?" It was approaching dusk. She didn't want Simon out alone in the cold, dark town.

"No, just a couple of blocks. What did he—"

"Simon, get your coat on then and head for home.

I need to have a talk with your father." She noticed that Henry carried a rifle. Did he always have it with him, or was he armed to hunt his missing son?

"Miss Douglas," Simon began, clearly upset with her.

"Is that all right with you, Mr. O'Keeffe? Will your son be safe walking home alone?" Melanie wouldn't press the point if Henry wasn't comfortable with it.

"Of course. There's nothing in this town more dangerous than a tumbleweed, and even they are frozen to the ground these days. I need to get supper. It's getting late."

"Let Simon head for home, then. I promise to be brief. You're right, it is getting late." She arched a brow at him and saw the man get the message.

"Run on home, Simon. I'll be two minutes behind you."

Simon took a long, hard look at Melanie, almost as if he wanted to stay and protect his pa.

"We won't be long, Simon." Melanie tilted her head toward the door. With a huff, Simon dragged on his coat and left the building.

Melanie knew then he was really worried because the door didn't even slam.

Chapter 3

Why did all the pretty women want to yell at him? Hank turned from watching Simon leave, then dropped his voice, not putting it past Simon to listen in.

"What's the problem, Miss Douglas?" Those snapping green eyes jolted him. He'd felt the jolt before, every time he'd gotten close to her in fact. And that surprised him because since Greta had died, no woman, no matter how pretty, had drawn so much as a whisper of reaction, let alone a jolt.

He'd gotten used to the idea that his heart had died with his wife. Melanie made him question that, but of course, all she wanted to do was yell at him. He braced himself to take the criticism. He deserved it.

"Mr. O'Keeffe, your son is a very bright boy. It's possible he's the smartest youngster in this school."

That wasn't what he expected to hear. Had she kept him here to compliment Simon? Maybe she wanted to pass Simon into a higher class? He *was* a bright boy. Hank felt his chest swell with pride, and he started to relax.

"But he is disrupting the whole school. We have to do something, between the two of us, to get him to behave."

Hank's gut twisted. It was fear. He tried to make himself admit it. But that effort was overridden by a need to fight anyone who spoke ill of his boy.

"You're saying you can't keep order in school?" Simon was all he had. Hank knew he didn't give the young'un enough attention, but a man had to feed his child, and that meant work, long hours of work.

"I was doing fine until today." Miss Douglas's voice rose, and she plunked her fists on her trim waist.

Hank looked at those pretty pink lips, pursed in annoyance. He'd never had much luck with women. He still had trouble believing Greta had married him. She'd seemed to like him, too, and it hadn't even been hard.

Now, when he needed to handle a woman right, calm her down, sooth her ruffled feathers, all he could think of was snapping at her.

He clamped his mouth shut until he could speak calmly. "What do you want from me, Miss Douglas? You want me to threaten him? Tell him if he gets a thrashing at school he'll get one at home?"

Hank didn't thrash Simon. Maybe he should.

Maybe sparing the rod was wrong, but the hurt in the boy since his ma died had made it impossible for Hank to deal him out more pain.

"I don't thrash my students, Mr. O'Keeffe. I have never found it necessary, and I don't intend to start now. What I want is—"

The schoolhouse door slammed open. "Hank, come quick, a fight broke out in the saloon."

Mr. Garland at the general store stuck his face in the room, then vanished. Hank took one step.

A slap on his arm stopped him. Miss Douglas had a grip that'd shame a burr.

"I'm not done talking to you yet." She'd stumbled along for a couple of feet but she held on doggedly.

"We're done talking. I have to go. My Simon is a good boy. You just need to learn to manage him better." He pried her little claws from his sleeve and managed to pull his coat open. "Let loose. You heard Ian. There's a fight."

"Why do you have to go just because there's a fight at the saloon?"

"I have to stop it."

"But why?"

His coat finally flapped all the way open, and he impatiently shoved it back even farther so she could see his chest.

And see the star pinned right above his heart. "Because just today I started a job as the town sheriff. That was the only way I could find a house in town. Now, if you can't handle one little boy, just say so and I'll get him a job running errands at the general store. Schoolin's a waste of time anyway for a bright boy like my Simon. Most likely the reason you can't handle him is he's smarter than you." A tiny smile curved his lips. "I got a suspicion he's smarter than me."

Then he turned and ran after Ian.

Chapter 4

About once a minute, while she closed up the school, put on her wrap, gathered up her books, locked the building, walked to Mrs. Rathbone's, and let herself in the back door, Melanie caught herself shaking her head.

"He's smarter than you."

There was no doubt in her mind that Simon was very bright. Was Mr. O'Keeffe right? Was it her fault?

"My Simon is a good boy, you just need to learn to manage him better."

Was it all about managing rather than discipline? She shook her head again. Not in denial, though there might be a bit of that, but to clear her head so she could think.

How long would Henry be dealing with that saloon fight? Simon was home, and he'd be expecting his father. Had Henry thought of that?

"You're finally here, Melanie?"

That cold, disapproving voice drove all thoughts of the O'Keeffe family from her head.

"Yes, Mrs. Rathbone." As if the old battle-ax ever had a thing to do with her. Melanie hadn't even gotten the back door closed before the woman started her complaining. Mrs. Rathbone had made it clear as glass that Melanie was to always use the back door, never the front—that was for invited guests, not school marms living on charity.

"I've eaten without you."

Melanie walked through the back entry and through the kitchen, where she picked up a plate, uncovered, sitting on the table, without a doubt cold and caked in congealed grease.

She walked down a short hall that opened onto an elegant dining room and on into a front sitting room. Mrs. Rathbone called it the parlor. She sat alone before a crackling fire, needlework in hand. She glanced up from the bit of lace she was tatting, peering over the top of her glasses, scowling.

"Good evening, Mrs. Rathbone."

The older woman sniffed. "A fine thing, a woman cavorting until all hours. The school board would not approve."

Always Magda Rathbone seemed on the verge of throwing Melanie to the wolves, ruining her career, and blackening her name with the whole town if she was forced to tell the truth of how poorly Melanie behaved.

Melanie happened to think she behaved with the restraint of a nun—a muzzled nun—a muzzled nun wearing a strait jacket. But no matter how carefully she spoke and how utterly alone she remained in the upper room, Mrs. Rathbone found fault.

"One of my students was left at school. His father is the new sheriff in town, and he was delayed. I minded the boy until his father could come."

"Hank O'Keeffe." Another sniff. "Everyone knows that boy of his is a terror, and as for Mr. O'Keeffe, he's got a lot of nerve being a lawman when he himself should be taken up on charges for the way he neglected his wife."

Melanie froze. What was this about Henry's wife?

"She'd still be alive if that man hadn't been so hard on her."

What sort of demands? Was she expected to work on the homestead? Or was there a darker meaning. Had Henry abused his wife? And was he now abusing his son?

"Go to your room now. I prefer quiet in the evening. Disturbances give me a headache."

Sent to her room like a naughty child. *I'll show you a disturbance you old battle-ax.* Melanie had a wild urge to start dancing around the room, singing at the top of her lungs. Disturbance? She'd show Simon a thing or two about disturbances.

Melanie, of course, did nothing of the sort. "Goodnight, Mrs. Rathbone."

"One more thing."

Melanie froze. She knew what was coming, the same thing that came every Monday morning, after Melanie had worked hard cleaning Mrs. Rathbone's house all weekend to earn her keep.

"Yes, ma'am?" What had the woman found to criticize now?

"I distinctly told you I wanted the library dusted this weekend. It's as filthy as ever."

The library. Two or three thousand books at least. And from what Melanie could see, judging by the undisturbed dust, Mrs. Rathbone had never read a one of them.

"I'll get to it, ma'am, but Sunday you specifically stopped me from dusting to clean out the cellar. There weren't enough hours this weekend to do both."

"You'd have gotten far more done if you hadn't spent a half a day idling."

"I spend half a day in church." Melanie squared her shoulders. She would never give in on this, even if it meant being cast into the streets in the bitter cold. "I will always spend Sunday morning attending services. I've made that clear, ma'am. In fact, the Lord's Day should be for rest. But I worked all afternoon and evening on the cellar."

Melanie clamped her mouth shut. Defending herself just stirred up the old harpy. And Melanie knew how miserably unhappy Mrs. Rathbone was. Her constant unkindness was rooted in her lonely life—a friendless existence shaped by her cruel tongue, a heart hardened to God, and her condemnation of anyone and everyone.

The people in Lone Tree endured Mrs. Rathbone, in part because of her wealth that she sprinkled onto the needs of the town, not generously, but she gave enough so that no one wanted to out-and-out offend her. Instead they avoided her and spoke ill of her behind her back.

It was a poor situation.

Melanie did her best to do as she was asked, even though the school board had said nothing about Melanie having to work as a housekeeper to earn her room. She suspected the board had no idea what was going on.

But it was a small town, most houses one or two rooms. There was nowhere else for Melanie to stay. She remembered what Mr. O'Keeffe had said about needing to take the job of sheriff to get a house. She had little doubt there were no empty houses in the raw little Nebraska town.

"I don't appreciate your tone. Get on to your room."

Because no *tone* could possibly come out of Melanie's mouth at this moment that would be appreciated, she went back to the kitchen, picked up the plate of food, and walked up the back staircase.

Melanie worked like a slave for Mrs. Rathbone at the same time being told she lived on charity. Each step she took upstairs wore on her as if the weight of the world rested on her shoulders.

The narrow stairs had a door at the bottom and top. Both were to be kept firmly closed, which also kept out any heat.

In Melanie's room, a chimney went up through the roof. It was the only source of heat—a chimney bearing warmth from two floors down.

It wasn't a small room; the attic stretched nearly the whole length of the house before the roof sloped. But Mrs. Rathbone had stored years of junk up here. There was barely room for Melanie's bed and a small basket with her clothing. She had to walk downstairs for a basin of water and bring it back up to bathe or wash out her clothing.

She spoke the most heartfelt prayer of her life,

asking God to control her temper with Mrs. Rathbone and with Simon and, while she was at it, with Henry. She prayed for strength sufficient for the day.

The prayers struck deep. Her impatience with Simon was sinful. It was easier to admit this now, with the boy away from her. While she was dealing with him, she felt justified in her anger.

Continuing to pray, she ate the unappetizing chicken—though it looked like it might have been good an hour ago. She swallowed cold mashed potatoes coated in congealed gravy. She was hungry enough she forced herself to eat every crumb of a piece of dried-out bread. She reached in her heart for true thankfulness for this food.

Only four days after Thanksgiving—a meal she'd cooked and served to Mrs. Rathbone, who had then told her to eat upstairs in her room. But Melanie knew she had plenty to be thankful for: first and foremost, a heavenly Father who loved her even if she was otherwise alone in the world.

She set her empty plate aside with a quick prayer of thanks that she wasn't hungry. She'd known hunger, and this was most definitely better. Turning her prayers to Simon, she remembered Henry's words: *"My Simon is a good boy. You just need to learn to manage him better."*

She begged God for wisdom to figure that out. If it was about managing Simon, then how did she do it?

Changing quickly into her nightgown in the chilly room, Melanie took her hair down and brushed it out, speaking silently to God all the while.

In the midst of her prayer, she remembered that moment earlier when she'd wondered about Simon going home alone tonight. She should have gone with him and stayed with him until his father arrived.

She worried enough about the trouble that little boy could get into alone that she was tempted to go make sure he was all right, though his father had to be home by now.

Her worry deepened along with her prayers as she set the hair combs and pins aside. Then her eyes fell on a large wooden box sitting on one of the many chests jumbled into the room. Strange that she'd never noticed it before, because right now it drew her eye so powerfully the dull wood seemed to nearly glow.

It was an odd little thing. Crudely made thing, the wood in a strange pattern, like a patchwork of little squares as if it had been put together with scraps of wood. About ten inches tall and as much deep and wide, a little cube. Four pairs of drawers were in the front, each with a little wooden knob. It wasn't particularly pretty, but there was something about it.

Her eyes went from the box to the combs and pins. They would fit in there perfectly. She should ask Mrs. Rathbone before she used the grouchy woman's things, but those little drawers seemed to almost beckon her.

With a shrug, Melanie decided she'd ask Mrs. Rathbone about the box in the morning, but for now, on impulse, she pulled open a drawer, which was much narrower and not as deep as she expected. Staring at the strangely undersized drawer, Melanie wondered at it for a moment, then slipped her hair things in.

A whisper of pleasure that made no sense eased the worst of her exhaustion and helped her realize the waste of energy worrying about Simon was at this late hour. Her chance to help was when Henry got called away. Now she was just letting sin gnaw at her mind and rob her of her peace.

The prayers and somehow the little box replaced her worry with a calm that could only come from God.

Prayer she understood, but why would a box do such a thing?

Chapter 5

Melanie asked about the box the next morning. Mrs. Rathbone snorted with contempt.

"I remember that shabby thing. It belonged to my husband's grandmother. His mother's mother. He adored that strange old lady and wouldn't part with any of her old keepsakes. That's what most everything is up in the attic. She was covered in wrinkles and dressed in the same old faded clothes, even though there was money for better. Those rags are probably still up in that attic, too. *Mamó* Cullen—that's what he called her—*Mamó*, what kind of name is that?"

An Irish word, most likely for mother or grandmother?

"She was ancient and blind by the time I came into the family and a completely selfish old woman. She seemed to be well into her dotage to me. The old crone seemed to never speak except to tell stories of the 'old country.' She always called Ireland 'the old country.' She was an embarrassment with her lower-class accent. I could hardly understand her. I hadn't met her before my marriage, or I might have had second thoughts."

Mrs. Rathbone waved a dismissive hand. "You can have that old box. I remember it well. My husband refused to part with it after his mother died. I'm not up to climbing all those stairs anymore. I'd forgotten it was up there or I'd have thrown it away by now. Now as to dusting the library. . ."

Melanie listened politely while Magda found fault. Being given the box lifted her spirits, and her prayers last night combined with her renewed determination to be thankful got her through breakfast and the packing of her meager lunch. The packing was done under Magda's watchful eye, lest Melanie become greedy and take two slices of bread.

Setting out for the short, cold walk to school before seven, Melanie feared Simon would be sitting there in the cold. He wasn't, but he appeared minutes later and came straight for the stove Melanie had burning.

The plucky thankfulness was sorely tested for the next eight hours. Simon started a fist fight, then two other boys ended up in a fight all their own. He tripped one of the older girls walking past his desk. The whole classroom erupted in laughter. During arithmetic he used his slate to draw a picture of a dog biting a man in the backside and passed it around the room to the wriggling delight of the other boys.

And through it all, the heightened noise and constant distraction, Simon hadn't learned a thing. And that was the worst of it. Neither Simon nor the other children were doing much work.

"My Simon is a good boy, you just need to learn to manage him better."

Manage him.

But how?

When the children were let out at twelve for lunch, they all ran home, except for Simon.

Her heart sank at the sight of him fetching a lunch pail and bringing it back to his desk. She'd planned for the noon hour to be spent in prayer that God would help her through the afternoon.

After eating his lunch far too quickly, Simon ran around the room—it was too cold to go outside. He complained and asked questions and just generally was as much trouble on his own as he was in the group. Instead of being able to sit in silence and listen for the still, small voice of God, she'd sent up short, desperate prayers for patience and wisdom—with no time to listen for God's answer.

He tore a page out of another child's reading book,

broke a slate, spilled ink—and then he lifted the flat wooden top of his desk into the air and dropped it with a clap so loud Melanie squeaked and jumped out of her chair.

Her temper snapped. "Simon why are you so careless?"

A sullen glare was his only answer.

Maybe if she threw him outside and told him to run in circles around the schoolhouse to burn off some energy.

"Hyah!" Simon dropped to his knees and shoved the desktop forward. He swung one arm wide like he was lashing an imaginary horse's rump and made a sound that was probably supposed to be a cracking whip.

Fighting to sound like it was a simple question, rather than the dearest dream of her heart, she asked, "Wouldn't you rather go home to eat?"

"Pa rides out to the homestead every day to do chores. We've got cattle out there. He can't get there, do his work, and get back in time to make a meal, so he packs a sandwich and milk for me."

The little boy had a better lunch than she did.

"Get off the floor and get to work putting your desk back together."

Simon stopped. "It was wobbly. I didn't take it apart on purpose."

He most certainly had.

"You have to stop taking things apart. Even if they're wobbly." It sounded like begging—and maybe that about described it. She was at her wit's end.

"It came apart on its own. I'll put it back together." His begrudging tone made it sound like she'd just told him his "horse" desktop had a broken leg and had to be shot.

"You took another desk apart, and you didn't get it put back together well. Which is why I moved you. Now this one will be wobbly, too, if you reassemble it poorly. I'll be out of desks by Friday."

"I'm going to get to work putting this back together right away."

"Is there a chance you can improve on yesterday's task?" Melanie heard the scold in her voice and fought to keep it under control.

Simon sat up straight. His eyes lit up.

Melanie nearly quaked with fear.

"I'll bet doing it a second time will help me improve. Once I'm done with this one, I'll work on the one from last night. This is good practice for me."

What did he mean practice? "Are you thinking of doing this sort of thing for a career, Simon?"

That was a form of teaching, she supposed.

"Yep. Pa's already given me a knife to whittle

with, and I've carved a toy soldier."

The thought of Simon with a sharp knife nearly wrung a gasp out of her.

"I'm going to keep at it until I've got an army." He was so enthused. "Then Pa's gonna show me how to build a toy-sized barn and a corral. He said pretty soon I'll be helping him build big buildings. We need a chicken coop come spring."

This excited him. "That is fine to learn a skill, but you're supposed to be studying reading, writing, and arithmetic while you're here at school. You shouldn't have time to practice your building skills."

Simon's face went sullen again. All the brightness and enthusiasm went out like a fire doused in cold water.

"Just get on with the desk, Simon. Maybe we can figure out a way you can work on your building skills after you're done with your studies." She tried to sound perky but all she could imagine in her future was one disaster after another.

Then a thought struck her. "Say, Simon, is your pa a good carpenter?"

"Yep, he built our sod house, and it's the best one all around."

The best house made of dirt. What a thrill.

"And he built a sod barn."

"Will the chicken coop be made of sod, too?"

Simon shrugged. "I reckon. Where would he get wood? There ain't no trees around. They didn't name this town Lone Tree for nothing."

Melanie thought of the majestic cottonwood that stood just outside of town. Alone. But the folks in town were planting trees. They'd tilled up the ground around the tree so seedlings had a fighting chance to sprout. Now little trees poked up every spring and were quickly transplanted. There were hundreds of slender saplings scattered around, but they were a long way from trees.

"Let's see if you can do a better job repairing this desk than you did last night. It will be a test of your skills. And please don't take anything else apart."

"But it was *wobbly*. It needed me to fix it."

Melanie decided then and there to impose on Mr. O'Keeffe and his admirable carpentry skills to keep the building standing—if working with sod translated to working with desks. What his son took apart, Mr. O'Keeffe could just reassemble.

And she'd start tonight because she wasn't going to let Simon go home to an empty house, no matter how late she had to stay at school. She'd felt the Lord telling her not to do that again.

Judging by last night, she could be here very late.

And wasn't Mrs. Rathbone going to have something to say about that?

Chapter 6

"Miss Douglas, Simon would be fine at home alone."

Melanie arched a brow at Henry O'Keeffe as she rose from beside the stove, where she'd been working on a desk, with Simon beside her. "He will stay here at school every day until you come for him. The only way to stop him from staying late is for you to get here at a reasonable hour."

She brushed at her skirt, and Hank suspected she had no idea what a mess she was. Her blond curls were about half escaped from the tidy bun she usually wore. Her hands were filthy. Her nose was smudged with grease or maybe ash. Something black was smeared here and there. She didn't seem aware of it or she'd have given up on smoothing her dress: that wasn't the worst of her problems.

Hank's temper flared, but he knew himself well. The temper was just a mask for guilt. Simon had spent too much time alone in his young life. The school marm was right.

"I can try and find someone around town who will let him come to their house after school. I know it's not fair to ask you to stay here with him. I apologize that you got stuck—"

"Mr. O'Keeffe," she cut him off.

Then she gave him a green-eyed glare he couldn't understand—except it was pretty clear she wanted him to stop talking.

There was a crash that drew both of their attention. Simon had just tipped over a bucket of coal, and black dust puffed up in the air around him.

"It is fine for him to be here. I enjoy his company." Her face twisted when she spoke as if she'd swallowed something sour. So she must not want him to say she was stuck with Simon. Which she most certainly was. Where did the woman get a notion that speaking the truth was a bad idea?

"Simon, clean up that coal and stay by the stove where it's warm. Miss Douglas and I need to speak privately for a moment." He clamped one hand on her wrist and towed her to the far corner of the room, which wasn't all that far in the one-room building.

She came right along, so maybe she had a few things to say, too. All complaints, he was sure.

"Mr. O'Keeffe—"

"Call me Hank, for heaven's sake." Hank enjoyed cutting her off this time. "It takes too long to say Mr. O'Keeffe every time."

"That would be improper."

She might be right, because Hank didn't know one thing about being proper. Dropping his voice to a whisper, he leaned close and said, "I'm sorry about this, but I work long hours and I see no way to run my farm and keep this job without working so long. And this job supplies us with a house in town—which we need because our sod house is too cold to live in through the winter."

She tugged against his hold and startled him. He hadn't realized he'd hung on. "You need to figure something out. Simon is running wild. He's undisciplined, and I think a lot of what he gets up to is a poorly chosen method of getting someone, anyone, to pay attention to him."

"He's just a curious boy."

A clatter turned them both to look at Simon, who had stepped well away from the coal bucket and was tossing in the little black rocks one at a time. A cloud of black dust rose higher with every moment, coating Simon and the room in soot.

To get her to look at him, so he could finish and get out of here, Hank gently caught her upper arm and turned her back to face him. "Things are hard when a man loses his wife and a boy loses his ma. I know we aren't getting by as well as we could, but that's just going to be part of Simon's growing-up years. Short of—" Hank dropped his voice low. "Short of letting someone else raise him, I don't know what else to do. And I won't give him up. I love my son, and his place is with me."

"Clearly, what you need to do, Mr. O'Keeffe—"

"Hank."

"No, Mr. O'Keeffe."

"No, Hank. Everyone here calls me that. Men and women both. Nebraska is a mighty friendly place, and you sound unfriendly when you call me Mr. O'Keeffe."

"Not unfriendly, proper."

"Call me Hank, or I'm going to start letting Simon sleep at school." Hank had to keep from laughing at her look of horror.

"Fine, Hank then. But—"

"He can stay then? Until I get done with work each night?" She'd offered. Her offer was laced with sarcasm and completely insincere, but it was too late to take it back now. Hank knew he was supposed to promise to get here on time, but he couldn't do any better than he had been doing, and besides, making those green eyes flash was the most fun he'd had in a long time.

She didn't disappoint him. Burning green arrows

shot him right in the chest. He got that same jolt he always got from her, and it occurred to him that he'd never had any idea what his wife had been thinking. Greta had always been a complete mystery.

Just thinking about it drew all the misery of living without her around him and all the fun went out of teasing Miss Douglas, who had never invited him to call her Melanie. Hank decided not to let that stop him. And if it annoyed her, all the better, because he needed her to stay away from him. He'd never again put himself in a position to face pain like he had when Greta died birthing their second child.

With that memory of pain, suddenly he couldn't wait to get away from the green-eyed school marm and her fault-finding ways.

"Let's go, Simon. We've kept Melanie here late enough."

Her gasp followed him as he rushed to get Simon, who was now in desperate need of a bath. They were gone before the bickering with Melanie could start up again.

∞

"Late again?"

You are a master of the obvious. "Good evening, Mrs. Rathbone. It's been a long day."

She waited. Maybe tonight would be the night Mrs. Rathbone would be agreeable. Or at least send her to bed with her supper and not a single word of criticism.

"If I told anyone on the school board that you're out at such a late hour, you'd be dismissed immediately. You are supposed to be a young lady of exemplary morals."

Melanie wasn't sure what the point was of that comment. She almost expected Magda to start blackmailing her.

"Split your thirty-dollar-a-month salary with me, or I will tell the school board about your sinfully late hours."

They wouldn't fire her. But Magda might kick her out of the house. Melanie wondered if the school board would object to her sleeping at the school. She was tempted to hunt them up and ask, but she knew it was improper for her to live alone, and sleeping at the school would certainly be alone. Unless, of course, Hank got any later, and Melanie started sleeping there with Simon. A woman and her—sort of—child could stay alone together.

If she walked away, Magda would call her back, upset at her impertinence. If she defended herself, Magda would only speak louder and become more critical. If she sat down to have a long, reasonable chat with the old bat, Magda would take offense at the familiarity of a woman living on charity thinking to sit with her as an equal.

Melanie suddenly couldn't stand it anymore, and she opened her mouth to tell the awful old woman to go ahead and report her. Melanie would sleep outside through a Nebraska winter before she'd take any more of this.

Then out of nowhere came her memory of that box. And with it came peace. Calm. How odd. She was able, without any trouble, to stand and take the harsh words Mrs. Rathbone handed out, and when the inevitable "go to your room" moment came, it was as easy as if the poor old lady had just politely said good-night.

"I'll see you in the morning, ma'am." Melanie turned away to the sound of an inelegant snort of disgust.

She picked up her supper, even colder than last night, and walked up to her room. The moment she entered, her eyes went to that box. What was it about that box that seemed an answer to prayer?

Even though that made no sense, Melanie knew it was true. She'd prayed for patience and that box had. . .had. . .glowed at her.

She ate quickly and removed the pins and combs from her hair, eager to put them away. Lifting the box from the trunk where it sat, Melanie sat on her bed, the closest the room had to a chair, and held the box in her lap.

Mamó Cullen. Melanie pictured an old Irish lady, wrinkled and full of charming stories of the old country. Was it possible Mamó Cullen hadn't been that thrilled with her new granddaughter-in-law and had, in fact, been unkind?

With a wry smile, Melanie knew that was entirely possible. She studied the odd box. The outside of it was full of seams, little squares of wood, some longer slats, and a few decorative brass knobs that didn't move when she tugged on them. There was nothing beautiful about it, but it was very old, and that alone made it charming.

Melanie slipped her pins and combs into the top drawer on the left. Then, on impulse, and because she really didn't want to put it down, Melanie pulled the little drawer all the way out and set it aside. Why was the drawer so small? She looked into the space where the drawer had been and saw solid wood. Then she pulled out the seven other drawers that went down the front of the box, each with a little brass knob just like those that didn't do anything. Each drawer was undersized. But this box wasn't heavy enough to be solid wood through and through.

Reaching in she touched the back of one drawer—playing with it, tipping the box sideways, holding it up to the lantern light so she could see the back, she touched and then pressed and thought the back gave just a bit. Not solid wood.

There had to be something in that unaccounted for space. She worked over the box for nearly an hour when she heard a little click and the back of one drawer slid sideways just a fraction of an inch. For a moment she thought she'd broken something, but looking in, she decided it wasn't broken, that piece was meant to move.

Finally she got it to slide farther, and that was accidental, too. She must have gripped something in just the right way, because the back of that drawer tipped forward, and Melanie could see it was on little hinges that showed when the cunning slat of wood fell flat. Something was in there.

Reaching, Melanie realized her fingertips trembled. She pulled a small scrap out, old, yellowed with age. A bit of cloth, no a delicate handkerchief, very fine and nearly a foot square when she brushed it flat.

It was embroidered in each corner with a piece of

a Nativity scene. Mary, Joseph, and the Baby Jesus in one corner. Two shepherds—one with a shepherd's crook and the other with a lamb around his neck—filled the next corner. Three wise men and a camel were in the third corner. In the fourth, in beautiful flowing script, stood the words "Peace on Earth."

The delicate stitches made each small picture a work of art. It was the most beautiful thing she'd ever seen.

Now that she knew how to open the one back, Melanie set to work on another and found it didn't work. The back had to come out, but not in the same way as the first. An idea sparked to life as surely as a match touched to a kerosene wick. An idea she knew was straight from God.

There would be something in each of these drawers. Almost certainly there would.

And finding them would be an activity to keep her. . .or better yet an over-active little boy. . .occupied for hours.

A little boy who loved carpentry.

With a sudden smile, she set the box aside and went to her reticule and found a copper penny and put it in the hidden space. She closed it up, packed the box in her satchel and made plans to lure her unmanageable little student into a quest.

As she lay down, she realized the next day was December 1. The beginning of the Christmas month. One of the first days in the season of Advent.

How many more drawers were there?

She'd have to find them before he did, and—judging by the size of the one drawer she'd found—she'd have to seek out tiny gifts to put in each.

Maybe Melanie could do more than bribe her little rapscallion into good behavior. Maybe with this Advent box, she could begin a journey to Bethlehem, to the Christ child, to a new, happier time for a sad and neglected little boy.

That was a lot to ask of an old, homely wooden box, but she couldn't help but believe that God was guiding her, and He would use her to guide Simon.

They'd do it together. One secret drawer at a time.

Chapter 7

Wednesday, December 1
The Fourth Day of Advent

Hank felt a chill slide up his spine that had nothing to do with the cold December evening. His son, sitting right next to Melanie Douglas, their heads bent over. . .something. Hank wasn't sure what.

Just as he stepped in, they looked at each other and shared the friendliest smile. It terrified him.

Melanie looked up, but he could tell she was reluctant. Whatever they were looking for had them both lassoed tight.

Her eyes focused on him, and that jolt hit. "Come on in, Hank."

Then she gave him that same friendly smile she'd shared with Simon. Up to now, she'd never been real friendly to him. This was the first time she'd called him Hank without an argument. The pleasure of it curved up his lips. They smiled at each other for too long, and Hank forgot all about his chilly backbone.

"You got here just in time, Pa." Simon sounded happier than he had since before Greta died.

"Just in time for what?" Hank decided then and there that whatever Melanie had done to make his boy this happy, he was going to encourage it.

"Look at this, Pa." Simon held up some dark thing about the size of a man's head. "I found a secret drawer."

Hank came toward the teacher's desk, trying to see what his son had.

Finally, when he got up close, he saw a stack of small wooden objects beside Simon. The knobs on them helped Hank figure out what he was looking at.

"Those are drawers you took out of this thing?"

"Yep, it's an Advent box, Pa."

"An Advent box, I've never heard of that."

"I just named it that because there are more drawers, maybe enough to last until Christmas. Simon will search for one each day after school." Melanie turned to Simon, and with mock severity waggled her finger under his nose. "If his school work is done."

Hank knew how curious Simon was and how much he liked working with his hands. He'd taken to whittling like he was born to it.

"And there was a present in the drawer I found,

Pa." Simon held up a penny. "Miss Douglas said it's a Christmas present for me. This box is full of secret drawers. And I have to stop disrupting class, too. Then I can spend the after-school time searching for another secret drawer."

Hank met those green eyes again. He was the one who'd challenged her to manage his son better. And she had come up with the perfect way.

"Can I see the box?" Hank grinned, unable to stop it. He wanted to search for hidden drawers, too. Melanie could probably make him behave and study with this box.

Simon and Melanie shared a conspiratorial smile.

Simon snapped something inside what looked like the opening for one of the drawers. "You try and find it, Pa."

Hank took the box before he noticed it was full dark. "I want to, but we've got to go home. We'll be late for supper as it is."

"Maybe you could try and get here a bit earlier tomorrow night, Hank." The asperity caught his attention; then he saw the sparkle of amusement in her eyes.

It widened his grin. "Maybe I can think of a way to get here. I wouldn't mind helping with the hunt." His hands tightened on the box, and he was surprised at how badly he wanted to sit down and search or maybe run off with the box and spend the evening with it.

Melanie snatched it from his hand. "I see that look. Simon had it, too. No, you may not take the box. The only way for Simon to spend time with it is to study and behave. And the only way for you to spend time with it, Hank, is to get here earlier. The rest of the time, this box is mine alone."

She tucked the box into a satchel that stood open on the desktop. "Well, it is time to close up for the day, gentlemen. I will see you early tomorrow morning, Simon. And you, Hank, I'll see perhaps late tomorrow afternoon."

Hank tugged on the brim of his Stetson. She had him caught just like a spider with a web. He'd work faster tomorrow, and he'd be here closer to school closing than he had been. And spend a bit of time with his son.

Chapter 8

Thursday, December 2
The Fifth Day of Advent

Melanie woke up exhausted the next morning. She'd stayed up terribly late last night. It took forever to find the rest of the drawers, and she had to do it before Simon did.

She'd managed to finagle each of the backs of the eight drawers open—none of them worked the same way—and she hoped the bright little boy didn't find a drawer she hadn't, because there'd be no gift.

With a smile she knew if he found an empty drawer, he'd just have to keep searching for the day anyway, and the gift wasn't the thing. It was the search. If he found a drawer she hadn't he'd probably crow with delight at having bested her.

Then she had to produce a small gift to put in each one. She had no opportunity to buy anything. She had to be at school by seven a.m. to beat her little friend's arrival and stay until nearly six at night waiting for Hank to come for him.

She had to come up with a few tiny gifts before Saturday, when finally she'd have a chance to go to the general store.

She looked among her own meager things—she hadn't left the orphanage for this job with many possessions.

Two things for Thursday and Friday. A little red pin, circular with a white cross painted on it. She'd earned this for perfect Sunday school attendance. She could find only one more thing small enough. A tiny, silver angel that she'd had all her life. At the orphanage she'd been told it was sewn into the hem of the little dress she'd been wearing when she was found left in a basket on a church doorstep.

The kind ladies who'd raised her kept it until she was old enough to care for it. It was her most treasured possession. Praying for a generous spirit, she thought of that unruly and loveable little Simon and smiled. It was easy to tuck the angel into the drawer.

If she thought of anything else to put in, and he didn't find this first, she might retrieve it. But where better to place an angel than in an Advent box?

As she left, with Mrs. Rathbone's nagging still ringing in her ears, she wondered if she should tell the old woman about the secret drawers. There was no question that Mrs. Rathbone had given her the box, but maybe if she knew about the hidden drawers, she'd want it back. After the first piece of embroidery, Melanie had found nothing in those drawers, and if she did, she would most certainly give anything she found to her landlady.

She'd spread the handkerchief on a flat surface to be a doily, and it felt as if she'd decorated for Christmas.

Melanie didn't ask. Simon was too excited about the box. What if Magda decided she did want it? Then what would happen to Simon and his behavior?

Melanie decided she'd wait until after Christmas to show Magda the hidden drawers. Though Melanie found herself loving the little chest, she'd return it to Magda if the woman wanted it.

~∞~

Monday, December 13
The Sixteenth Day of Advent

"Have you found a new one yet?" Hank found himself nearly running during the day to get all his chores done. And he could have stayed longer at the farm and walked a patrol around the town to make sure everyone knew the sheriff was on duty. But he loved helping Simon and Melanie play with that box.

And each hidden space was harder to find. He had a feeling the hard part was just beginning.

"Hi, Pa." Simon lit up. "I've been hunting a while, but we've found all the easy ones."

"The easy ones?" Hank laughed as he hung up his coat and hat.

At the sight of his son's cheerful welcome, Hank kept a smile on his face, but honestly he wanted to kick his own backside. How many times had he been too busy to make sure his son was happy?

"Those hidden spaces in the backs of the drawers weren't easy."

Simon laughed, and Melanie's sweet, musical laughter joined in. She was so pretty. Hank pulled a chair up to the desk on Simon's right while Melanie sat on the boy's left. He'd brought the chairs over the third day they'd worked together, before that there'd only been Melanie's teacher's chair in the schoolhouse.

Simon turned the box so the side with the drawers lay face-down on the table. "The whole back half is still not open, Pa. The drawers and spaces behind 'em don't come close to taking up all the space." Simon held the box up so it was between them, his eyes intent as he examined the back.

"These thin slats of wood must open." Hank

wanted to grab the box and push and slide those slats. Instead he let his son work on it. Hank quietly pointed here and there, making suggestions.

"Try sliding two at a time. Remember that one hidden compartment that only opened when all the other compartments were closed and the drawers were back in place, except for the one we were working on?" Melanie reached for the box, checked herself, and pulled her hand back. Hank laughed quietly and looked up at her.

"Hard to be patient, huh?"

She laughed.

"Thanks for letting me find them." Simon looked up. Hanks's son's blue eyes gleamed as bright as a guiding star.

"Get back to work." Hank jabbed a finger at the box, but he smiled all the way from his heart. A heart that'd felt more dead than alive for the last two years. "It ain't easy to be so generous."

Melanie laughed. Simon joined in, then bent his head back to the box, still chuckling. The boy focused intently on the job—but with a smile on his face.

Melanie brushed a yellow curl off her cheek and tucked it behind her ear in a move so graceful Hank could've sworn he heard music. She rested a hand on

Simon's head with an amazingly motherly gesture. Hank looked up and met Melanie's green gaze. She quietly snickered and smoothed Simon's unruly black curls.

Her laughter, the affectionate touch, the change in his boy, the few inches that separated them, all hit Hank in a different way than the usual jolt.

Something so deep, so strong.

He cared about her, and not in a way that had anything to do with a good teacher who'd found a way to manage an unruly student. The feeling had nothing to do with Simon at all.

He cared about her. He knew he could love her.

Their eyes held. The moment stretched. Hank felt himself lean closer. With Simon here, he couldn't think of kissing her but—he was thinking of kissing her.

He was drawn to her warmth and heat. She leaned his direction, just an inch, two inches, three. He lifted his hand to rest it on top of hers, still caressing Simon's hair.

When he touched that soft, smooth skin, he remembered Greta. They'd been this close, with Simon between them, as she died, their unborn child forever trapped inside her.

He'd touched her just this way. Simon, her hand,

his. And felt the life go out of her. Seen the moment her eyes had lost vitality. Her hand had slid from Simon to the bed, and all Hank's love couldn't hold her. As she lay dying in childbirth, he felt as if his love had killed her.

Pain like he'd never known swept over him. He'd barely survived losing her. In a lot of ways he hadn't survived—neither had Simon. They'd stayed alive, but there was no life in either of them, no joy, no family, no love.

And now here he was touching another woman. He would *never* put himself through that much pain again.

Only a fool risked that. He didn't know what went across his face, but right there, with Simon so intent on the Advent box that they might as well have been alone, her spark of laughter died. Her hand slid from between Hank's hand and Simon's head, just as Greta's had.

She looked down and brushed some bit of nothing off her dress and cleared her throat. "I need to spend a little time getting tomorrow's lesson together."

"No, Miss Douglas," Simon looked up from the box, wheedling. "Stay and help."

"Let me get a few things done for the Christmas

program practice for tomorrow. I ask you to do your work before you can work on the Advent box, so it's only fair I behave by the same rules. " Melanie reached, froze, then almost as if she couldn't stop herself she brushed Simon's dark, over-long hair off his forehead. His curls flopped back right where they had been.

"I'll come back as soon as I'm finished." She smiled at Simon, too decent to let the boy see she needed to get away. "In the meantime, you and your pa work together."

He'd hurt her to protect himself. A shameful thing for a man to do.

Simon let her go without an argument. And Simon hadn't done anything without an argument in two years. His tears had dried after Greta's funeral and he'd started causing trouble. And Hank had found enough work so that he could avoid dealing with his troublesome son.

Only since Melanie had Hank been able to see a ray of hope that his son might stop being such an angry youngster. So, he'd thank her for it and thank God for bringing such a good teacher into town, but he would not let any feelings for her take root.

She moved away, and he focused on this strange

box-full-of-secrets. As he studied it, he wondered if he was like this box. Full of hidden places.

Guarded, impossible to open unless someone worked really hard.

Hank decided he liked it that way. He would open enough to let his son in, but no more. And just as well, because what woman would work so hard for the doubtful pleasure of finding all the private places in Hank's heart, especially if he hurt them when they got close?

With regret, but feeling far less afraid, he went back to working with Simon. They were at it for a long time, completely lost in testing each and every piece of wood in every way they could think of. Then while he held a small slat of wood that sprung back into place whenever they let it go, Simon tipped the box on its side and they heard a faint click. Hank's eyes rose and met his son's.

"Did you hear that, Pa?" Simon almost vibrated with excitement.

It hit Hank hard that Simon had been sitting still, working hard, showing great patience for a long time. Hank had, too. He remembered how hard it'd been for him to stay in his desk when he was a sprout. One of these days he ought to tell Simon he was a pretty normal child. In looks Hank and

Simon were a match, but it appeared that they were a match inside as well.

For now, Hank smiled at his boy; then the two of them turned back to the box. Simon went right back to his diligent work, but it only took a couple of seconds for him to slide one of the thin boards on the back. It slid all the way out and revealed a skinny compartment, as tall as the box but less than an inch deep. And inside the little space was—

"Miss Douglas, it's a tin soldier." Simon's voice shook with excitement. He'd been whittling, and he'd made a little soldier. Hank knew the boy had plans to build his own army. Now he could add this little tin man to it. The soldier shone in the lantern light, and that's when Hank realized it had gotten dark. Every day was shorter as they closed in on the first day of winter.

"Miss Douglas, come and see." Simon lifted up the toy. Hank realized, not for the first time, that Simon didn't understand where these toys came from. The boy thought they were just there, maybe miraculously, put there by God as Christmas gifts.

Melanie hadn't taken credit for the gifts herself.

She came close, her attention all on Simon, and smiled at the intricately shaped toy. "That's beautiful. Didn't you say you were whittling a toy soldier?"

"Yep and now I've got two. By the time I'm done, I'm going to have a big enough army to protect everyone.

Hank wanted that, too, a way to protect everyone.

But first Hank had failed his wife. Then by neglect, he'd failed his son. Now he was busy protecting himself from another broken heart.

Did that mean for once he was doing right by protecting himself? He looked at Melanie, who'd never spared him a glance, and wondered if instead it meant he was failing again.

Chapter 9

"And don't think I won't talk to the school board!"

Melanie could usually remain calm, but the way Hank had looked at her tonight—as if he wanted her as far away from himself as possible—had shredded her normal calm. She'd prayed almost desperately while she tried to find something to do to keep busy until Hank and Simon left.

In the end, she'd rewritten some of the lines of the play, sewn hems in two costumes, worked on some decorations she wanted the children to finish, and read through the highest level arithmetic book she had, a book she was familiar with and understood completely.

Through it all, she prayed.

Memories of the years at the orphanage haunted her and seemed tied to that look in Hank's blue eyes. She'd always borne this heavy feeling there was something wrong with a little girl who had no parents, an older child who was never adopted, a young woman who'd never found a man to love her.

She didn't have those thoughts so much anymore.

Living alone in an attic and working all day with children, she was too busy or too alone to be rejected.

Until now. By Hank.

"I know you're spending time in that schoolhouse—alone with a man. There's talk all over town."

Melanie had to dig deep to find the calm needed to keep from snapping back at Magda's verbal assault. Every day it was harder to turn the other cheek, to return good for Mrs. Rathbone's evil. And today—thanks to Hank—holding her tongue was harder than ever.

"Simon is there, Mrs. Rathbone. We're certainly not spending time alone, and Hank, uh, that is Mr. O'Keeffe is often occupied with his work as sheriff. I won't send a little boy home to an empty house. I'm trying to get Simon more interested in school work and less interested in causing trouble. And he's doing very well. Often when Hank gets there, Simon is in the middle of something. . . ." *Trying to open hidden compartments in the box you gave me, which I should tell you about. But I don't dare, for fear you'll take it from me.* "I hope a few more nights"—twelve: there were twelve more days until Christmas—"and Simon won't need extra help anymore."

The Advent box in her satchel seemed to weigh more with each passing moment. Melanie felt heat climbing up her neck, and she knew she had to get upstairs before she said something that got her thrown out of this house—the only available home for her in town.

"One word from me to the parson and the doctor and Mr. Weber at the general store," Magda rattled off the names of the men on the school board, "and I can blacken your name to the point you'll be fired." Mrs. Rathbone waggled a finger from her chair by the warm fire.

"And it's a wonder I can breathe with the dust you kicked up cleaning the library last weekend."

"I'll dust the rest of the house this weekend, ma'am." Prayer. Melanie clung to prayer.

God don't let me shame myself with my foolish temper. I need this home. Surround me with protection from this enemy.

"I won't have a woman of questionable character in my home. No Christian woman should have to put up with it."

Melanie knew it was either run or say something absolutely dreadful. Terrible, sinful words burned in her throat, and it wasn't even Mrs. Rathbone's fault. All of her need to rage could be laid right at the feet of Hank O'Keeffe because of his withdrawal from her.

She chose to run. "Good-night, Mrs. Rathbone."

Grabbing her plate, ignoring Mrs. Rathbone's insistent demand to come back, she rushed up those cold stairs. Every day the weather was worse. Melanie had been able to see her breath in the room when she got dressed this morning.

Today was Monday, and the weekend had allowed Melanie to find a few more drawers in the box, but she knew the strange object still held some unaccounted-for space. She'd become nearly obsessed with finding them all. She'd bought enough tiny toys and candy to last until Christmas; whether the hidden compartments would last that long, she didn't know.

Of course, she only had to find enough drawers to keep Simon busy on school days. A smile crossed her lips as she remembered Simon sidling up to her at church to plead for a look at the box right then.

The little pill was as eager as she was.

Melanie gained her room, set her plate on the bed, drew the Advent box out of her satchel, and set it on the trunk. She studied it and felt led to pray as she ate her cold meal.

The entire center of the box was still unexplored.

The little drawers on the front and back were accounted for. . .by her. Simon still had a while to go finding them.

The meal was decent enough, if a girl had spent her entire life in an orphanage with a meager budget. She finished it quickly and picked up the box. She'd been listening for that click as Simon and Hank worked.

She'd been all weekend finding it herself.

Now which of the many little seams between wooden slats and tiles was the one that needed to be tipped just so, pressed just so. . . Often two things moved at the same time. . .

At last, because she'd learned tipping the box made a difference, Melanie finally pushed the right boards with the box tilted at the perfect angle, and the whole box popped. A seam appeared right down the middle, separating the front with the visible drawers from the back with the other compartments they'd found. Hinged on one side, she found more little tiles and slats of wood. But a grin broke across her face. She was learning how this strange box worked. There were little nooks and crannies to be found all over in this new section.

Not easy, because nothing about the Advent box was easy. But findable. She could do it. Simon could do it. And very possibly, just based on the small sizes of the drawers they'd found up until now, there might be enough spaces to last until Christmas.

After that, she'd tell Mrs. Rathbone about the little drawers, and if the contentious old lady agreed to let Melanie keep it, she'd give it to Simon as a Christmas gift.

The discovery of the new stash of drawers helped set aside the hurt from Hank. Well, not set it aside really, just accept it. More pain in a life that had dosed her with a lot of it. Nothing new, not even a surprise.

She got ready for bed with a prayer of thanks in her heart.

Chapter 10

Tuesday, December 14
The Seventeenth Day of Advent

They found several slender lengths of wood painted bright red.

"What's this, Miss Douglas?"

Hank looked at Melanie, who was busy writing, always working on her Christmas play. Or so she said.

With a sweet, sad smile that made Hank's heart ache—because he'd put that sadness there—she shook her head. "I don't know. What do you think it could be?"

She did a very good job of acting mystified.

It had been left to Hank to notice the little slots that fit together to form an outlined A-frame building.

⚬∾⚬

Wednesday, December 15
The Eighteenth Day of Advent

"It looks like a little ball of yarn, Pa." Simon's brow

furrowed as if he had no idea what to make of a knotted up ball of yarn.

Hank noticed Melanie lean a bit toward them from where she sat by the pot-bellied stove, with a pair of knitting needles and a ball of white yarn.

"Look closer, son. It's got a little red nose and two blue knots for eyes. And these little sticks are legs. It's a lamb."

Simon had brought the strange little A-frame sticks with him and suddenly Hank knew what it was.

"The sheep goes in the barn, only it's a stable, like the stable in Bethlehem."

Melanie eased back in her chair without comment and went back to her knitting.

∞

Thursday, December 16
The Nineteenth Day of Advent

"It's a star." Simon's voice rang with excitement. He knew now what was coming. The stable, the sheep, the star.

Hank watched as Simon examined it. The star was sewn with felt and just the tiniest bit padded like a tiny star-shaped pillow. It was stitched onto a button, the whole thing painted bright yellow. Melanie had made this with her own hands, just like the sheep.

A loop of thread on the button was perfect to hang the star on a little notch on the stable. Hank hadn't noticed that notch until just now.

What else had she made? There had to be an entire Nativity scene coming. Each of the few pieces were clever. But how did she make the people? She should have come to him. But of course he'd made it impossible.

He looked over, and her gaze met his. He got his jolt for the day. Then she looked back at the piece of white fabric she was cross-stitching. She wasn't even pretending to be busy with schoolwork anymore.

∞

Friday, December 17
The Twentieth Day of Advent

Simon squealed over the tiny piece of carved wood. It was Mary the Mother of Jesus. Hank knew then what she'd done. He'd seen these figures in the general store and had never given them a second thought. For one thing their price was a bit dear. But Melanie had bought the set, and now they'd be introduced to the Holy Family one at a time.

Family. Hank rested his eyes on Melanie. Her head bent over her work. How he'd loved having a real family.

❧

Monday, December 20
The Twenty-third Day of Advent

A little donkey.

"Donkey's are stubborn things, ain't they, Pa?"

"It's *aren't*, Simon, not *ain't*. You must use proper grammar." Melanie's voice drew Hank's attention, as if he wasn't already paying too much attention to her.

"They are stubborn, Simon," she said. "Almost as stubborn as men."

Melanie's lips quirked in a smile. A real smile. He detected no sadness. But the smile was gone, and she didn't look up.

He needed to find a way to make her look up. He needed his daily dose of her pretty eyes.

❧

Tuesday, December 21
The Twenty-fourth Day of Advent

"Was Joseph Jesus's father or was God?" Simon studied the little bit of wood, perfectly painted, about as tall as his little finger.

"Well, God was Jesus' real Father, but Joseph was like the father God gave him here on earth."

"Like Mike Andrews has a new pa? I hear Mike call him a stepfather, but he acts just like a regular pa."

"I don't know if Joseph is exactly Jesus' stepfather, because that's what you get when your own pa is dead and Jesus' heavenly Father was with Him in spirit."

"Is Ma with us in spirit, Pa?"

Hank looked down at Simon and saw only curiosity. No hurt. He probably could barely remember Greta. Hank's thoughts faltered because for a few seconds he couldn't picture her. Couldn't bring her face to mind. Then it came back to him, Greta's face. But he pictured her as his young bride. Happy, working hard, a good cook, a pretty woman with a nice singing voice and a tendency to nag. She was usually right, so Hank didn't hold that against her.

He realized that he'd always before pictured her as she was when she was dying. In pain, ashen white, bleeding. But now the good memories came flooding in and replaced the bad. He felt a part of his heart heal.

And he looked at Melanie, who for once didn't have her eyes fixed on her work. She watched Simon with concern and kindness. Maybe afraid Hank would say some boneheaded thing that made Simon feel bad.

"She is indeed, Simon. But that isn't exactly how it was with Jesus being God's Son." Hank told Simon the Christmas story in a way that was more real than the usual reading from the Bible. Precious as those words were, talking with his son, discussing a heavenly Father, a stepfather, a mother who'd died, the story of Jesus was more real to Hank than it had ever been. And he owed that to Melanie.

He looked up at her as he talked, and for once she smiled at him as she had before he'd driven her away from the desk and the Advent box.

She'd never by so much as a tone in her voice punished Hank for his harsh rejection.

‿∞‿

Wednesday, December 22
The Twenty-fifth Day of Advent

"Melanie, come over and see what we found." Hank didn't betray himself, but Melanie looked up, and her eyes flashed.

"What is it?" She knew good and well what it was. She'd put it there.

"Come and see, Miss Douglas." Simon sounded excited, and Hank knew that however unhappy Melanie might be with him, she'd not deny Simon her attention.

Rising with great reluctance, she set aside her needlework and came to the desk to see Simon hold up the tiny angel. Hank had no idea where she'd gotten this.

But he couldn't ask without letting Simon know she'd put it in there. He was willing to believe this box was just for him, maybe the gifts put there by God. Hank wasn't sure just what his son thought about this box, only that he loved it, was fascinated by it, and that as he'd opened the secret drawers, he'd also opened his heart. Hank had regained his son's love. And he'd have never done it without the generous school marm.

"It's an angel, Melanie." Hank didn't take it from Simon; he'd have had a tug of war. But he lifted Simon's hand and turned it a bit so the angel shone in the lantern light. This drawer had taken hours to find. Hank couldn't believe how well Simon had learned to concentrate and stick with a task.

Rising from his chair he stepped around his son so he was just that little bit closer to Melanie. "An angel put in this box by an angel."

Melanie looked past Hank to Simon. But his son was busy finding the perfect place for the angel in his nearly complete Nativity set.

Hank touched her arm and gained her full

attention. "Thank you, Melanie. And I'm sorry I've made it so you"—he dropped his voice to a whisper—"couldn't help. So sorry. God bless you for letting Simon and me take this journey to Christmas together. But I'd like it if you joined us. I let fear and my grief push you away, but I've found my way past it now. I have you to thank for it and, if you'll forgive me, please help us, these last two days before Christmas, search for the last drawers."

Melanie looked scared, like a woman might who'd been hurt too many times. But she nodded. "I'd like that. Thank you."

∽

Thursday, December 23
The Twenty-sixth Day of Advent

When they opened the next little cranny, Simon said, "It's a baby Jesus."

He reached his chubby little fingers into the ridiculously well-hidden spot and pulled out a tiny baby in a manger. Hank wasn't too surprised. His eyes went to the little Nativity scene set up on Melanie's desk. Simon brought them every day and set them up before he started hunting.

"Pa, it's just like when Jesus was born." Simon looked up and smiled. All of the pain his boy had carried for two years seemed to be gone. Hank was at fault that the boy had been so unhappy. He'd blamed it on Greta's death, but spending this time with Simon had shown Hank the truth.

And it was because of Melanie's wisdom that they'd come so far, taken a journey just as the Holy Family had.

Smiling, uncritical, Simon asked. "But what's left now? Finding the baby Jesus should have happened Christmas Day."

Hank didn't know. Had Melanie hoped they wouldn't find Jesus until tomorrow? Christmas day was Saturday. But the Nativity was completed. What else could there be?

And though she'd joined them in their search today, after he'd asked her to forgive him, she hadn't steered them. They found whatever they found. So, it's possible this wasn't the order she'd hoped the compartments would be opened.

He looked at her, and she was watching Simon, smiling. Not a flicker of alarm that they'd found the wrong drawer.

"Let's go ahead and put Jesus in by Mary and Joseph." Melanie and Simon turned to arrange all the little figures.

While they did it, Hank, his hands moving idly

on the box did something and a new drawer popped open. A drawer Hank could see had nothing in it. The oddest little slit in the wood. She hadn't found it yet. He knew if she had there'd be some bit of a thing in there.

But this drawer, well, Hank knew exactly what belonged in this one. He took a second to study the cunning little space before he snapped it shut.

And then he made his plan while Melanie and Simon talked about the first Christmas.

∽

Thursday, December 24
The Twenty-seventh Day of Advent

Melanie lined the children up to sing their final song. They were so bursting with Christmas cheer it had been hard to get them to do their parts, but in the end, with a few funny mix-ups, they'd done a wonderful job.

When the school finally was almost emptied out, she smiled at the two who remained. She'd asked Magda's permission to keep the box, even opened a few of the little drawers. Magda had waved it off as if it smelled bad.

"Simon can you come here, please?" As always, Simon came rushing up, eager to search. But tonight

168

there was to be no search.

She reached under her desk to get her satchel. "It's gone." She straightened to see Hank holding the box.

"I wanted to look at it closer." He handed it to Melanie.

"We've found all the drawers but I do have one final gift for you."

She extended the Advent box to him. "This is for you and your pa." Her eyes raised to Hank.

"It's mine?" Simon gasped, then grabbed the box and hugged it, his face beaming with joy.

"Yes, Merry Christmas."

Hank stood beside her, both of them facing Simon.

The sweet little boy set the box down. "I'm going to open every little compartment just for the fun of it."

"Simon, it's too late. We can't—"

"Let him work on it for a while, Melanie."

Melanie saw a look pass between the two and wondered at it.

The warmth of Hank's voice drew her eyes from the boy to the man. Hank rested one strong hand on Melanie's arm. Smiling, knowing he wanted space between them and Simon so they could talk, she let him pull her over to the stove. All of ten feet away from the distracted child.

"Melanie," Hank rested both hands on her upper arms. His blue gaze locked on hers, and it drew her in just as his hands drew her closer.

"Y—yes?" She hoped that yesterday had changed things between them. But she was a woman who had learned so long ago not to hope.

"Melanie, it's taken me too long. I've been stubborn, and mostly I've been afraid. But I'm not afraid anymore."

His voice charmed her. His hands, so strong, could protect her from the whole world. Oh yes, she wanted to hope.

His head lowered. His lips touched hers.

The first kiss of her life. The sweetest kiss she could imagine.

"Melanie, that box has one more secret to tell."

"What?"

Then he kissed her again, and she didn't care much about that box, no matter how it had taken them on a journey to find each other.

"There!" A harsh voice shocked Melanie out of the romantic daze, and she jerked her head toward the schoolhouse door.

"I demand she be fired." Mrs. Rathbone stormed into the schoolhouse with the parson, the doctor, and Mr. Weber right behind her.

Parson Howard arched a brow. "Hank, what's going on?"

"That's a stupid question, Parson." Doc Cross smiled at Melanie.

Mr. Weber alone looked shocked. "I can see how upsetting this is to you, Magda. Of course, we can't keep a young lady who'd behave so scandalously working here."

"What?" Melanie needed a job.

"And she won't sleep another night under my roof."

Gasping, Melanie said, "It's snowing out and bitter cold. And you'd throw me out of your home?"

"And what's more she's a thief."

"Thief?" Melanie cried. "I am not a thief."

"What about that box?" Mrs. Rathbone jabbed a finger at the box just as Simon came up beside her, holding it, its many hidden drawers now wide open.

"But you told me I could have it. I asked again this morning."

"You did no such thing. You're a thief and a liar. Mr. Weber, Hank can't be trusted to do the sheriff's job. Please take over."

The fear that swept through Melanie nearly choked her. Mrs. Rathbone was just spiteful enough to demand Melanie be arrested.

Simon stormed right up to Mrs. Rathbone.

"No, Simon, come back." Melanie remembered in a flash all the changes that had come over Simon in the last month. But now he nearly quaked with anger. If he believed Melanie had lied and stolen— for heaven's sakes, stolen a gift for him—would it undo all the good Melanie had done?

He shoved the box right at Mrs. Rathbone's ample belly. "Here, take the box. Miss Douglas isn't a thief. But if you want it back, you can have it."

Magna caught the box by reflex, then gave it a distasteful look. Melanie knew the old bat didn't want that box. She just wanted to cause trouble. Walking in on a kiss was one good way to accomplish her goal. Had the woman agreed Melanie could have that box with the plan of accusing her of theft? Or had the woman just seen it in the schoolhouse and seized on another accusation.

With one quick move, Hank snatched the box out of Magda's hands.

Mrs. Rathbone squawked like an angry rooster.

"You can have it back in just a minute." Hank looked at the three men standing a step behind her. "And you can all just stay right here for a while longer. I think I can clear all this up."

"I'd appreciate it if you would," Doc Cross said with weary amusement that didn't match the emotional temperature of this upsetting meeting. "And be quick about it. My wife is holding supper."

Hank turned with the box and brought it to Melanie. He let go of it with one hand and touched Simon's shoulder. "Stay right here with me, Son. This is from both of us."

"You can't give her that box as a gift, it's mine." Magda was still storming around.

"I won't give her the box." Hank manipulated two boards while holding the box nearly on its side and the slot tipped open.

"Reach in. Today it was my turn to bring a gift for you."

Melanie saw the sincerity in his eyes and slowly reached in the tiny dark gap he'd opened. She grasped something and pulled it out. "A ring."

Nodding, Hank said, "A wedding ring. Marry me, Melanie. You have no home to go to, so we can marry and you'll come home with me."

Her stomach sank as she heard the practical reasons she should marry. And a lonely child who'd never been loved couldn't help noticing he hadn't said the one thing she wanted above all to hear. "Th—that isn't a good reason to get married."

"Then just marry me because I love you."

She gasped in delight. Hank leaned down and caught that gasp with his kiss. He pulled back. "Say yes, Melanie, marry me. Then let's finish this Advent journey we've been on. Let's end it at our home."

Hank's hand left her arm to rest on Simon's head. The little boy grinned up at her in what looked like glee. "Marry us, Miss Douglas. We love you."

Melanie couldn't stop the grin that spread across her face, though so many looked on and she'd been accused of terrible things.

"Yes, I'll marry you." She looked at sweet Simon. Then her eyes lifted to meet Hank's gaze. She couldn't look away. "I'll marry you for one reason only, Hank. Because I love you, too."

Hank turned to face the four people who'd witnessed his proposal. He handed the now-empty box back to Mrs. Rathbone. "You can have that, ma'am."

Magda looked at it with a scowl. "Oh, just keep the ugly old thing." She slammed it onto a desktop and walked out in a huff.

"Parson, as long as you're here, will you say some vows and give us your blessing?" Hank asked. "And Doc, Mr. Weber, will you be witnesses?"

Both men grinned. Doc Cross said, "Make it quick, Parson, my wife is a fine cook."

They said their vows, and Melanie received the finest gift of all. The gift of being an Advent bride.

Hank slid the ring on Melanie's finger at just the right time. Simon hugged the Advent box tight. Then the three of them walked home.

Just as Mary and Joseph, on that long-ago Christmas, had completed their Advent journey, now Melanie, Hank, and Simon completed theirs: a journey that brought them to Christmas, to family, to love.

About the Author

Mary Connealy writes romantic comedy about cowboys. She is a Carol Award winner, and a Rita, Christy, and Inspirational Reader's Choice finalist. She is the bestselling author of the Wild at Heart series, which recently began with book number one, *Tried & True*. She is also the author of the Trouble in Texas series, Kincaid Bride series, Lassoed in Texas Trilogy, Montana Marriages Trilogy, Sophie's Daughters Trilogy, and many other books. Mary is married to a Nebraska rancher and has four grown daughters, and three spectacular grandchildren. Find Mary online at www.maryconnealy.com.

The Nativity Bride

by Miralee Ferrell

Chapter 1

Goldendale, Washington
September, 1875

A pillow connected with Curt Warren's backside, and he staggered but caught himself. "Where did you come from, Deb? I didn't even see you there." He raised his down-filled pillow above his head and ran across the Summers' kitchen after sixteen-year-old Deborah Summers as her laughter filled the air.

"You may have longer legs than me, Curt, but I'm quicker." She darted to the side of the wood stove, her breath coming in gasps, then raced out again to cover the expanse of the room and slipped into their dining area, where she skidded to a halt, her pillow raised in defense. "I got the last lick in, so I win."

"Who says we're done?" He frowned in mock anger and inched forward, hoping she wouldn't notice.

She giggled and sidled the opposite direction. "Your father, that's who. He's expecting you home to do chores, and you know how grumpy he gets if you're late. Admit it, you don't want to get beaten by a girl, even if it's a girl you're sweet on." She arched a sassy brow and winked.

Curt tossed the pillow onto a chair, and as her gaze followed it, he lunged forward and grasped her upper arms before she could scamper away. "A girl I'm sweet on, huh? Let's just see about that." As quick as a hummingbird swooping for nectar, he dipped his head and attempted to steal a kiss, but the little minx turned her head, and his lips landed on her cheek. "Ah, Deborah, come on. Just one little kiss before I go?"

She squealed, but didn't try too hard to get away. She put her hand on his chest and pushed, smirking as she did so. "I didn't hear you say you're sweet on me, and we're not betrothed yet, so no kisses for you."

She danced across the floor and waved her hand toward the door. "It's a good thing Ma's upstairs on the far end of the house or you'd have waked her by now. You'd best get before your pa comes looking for you." Her pretty face sobered. "Will I see you tomorrow when you're done with chores?"

"Yep, I reckon you will, as long as Pa doesn't keep me till after dark." His heart thudded at the quirk of Deborah's lips. If only he could kiss her! He rolled his eyes as she pointed at the door again. "All right, I'm going. You don't have to shove me out, you know."

"From the expression I glimpsed a second ago, I think I do." Her smile faded, and she ducked her head. "I'll see you tomorrow."

He eased toward the door then pivoted after he grasped the knob. "I love you, Deborah." He jerked on the knob and bolted down the steps, not waiting for her reply. He believed she felt the same, but he wasn't taking any chances. As soon as she turned seventeen, he'd ask her to marry him.

Curt raced across the fields that connected his father's farm with the Summers', then slowed his pace as he neared the barn. Hopefully Pa would still be in the east pasture. He slipped inside, waiting a minute for his eyes to adjust to the dim light, then groaned. The cows were already in their stations, ready to milk.

Pa stepped around a corner and glared. "You're late. Bringing in the cows is your job."

"I know, Pa. I'm sorry." He grabbed a milk pail and pulled up the milking stool.

"You need to stop seeing Deborah." Pa crossed his arms over his chest and kept his eyes riveted on Curt. "The way you're going, you'll ruin her life. You aren't interested in this farm, and all you want to do is play. Maybe it's time you figured out what you *do* want to do."

Curt stared at his father, certain he hadn't heard correctly. "What?" He shook his head. "I love Deborah, and there's no way I'm going to stop seeing her. I can't believe Ma feels the same way."

Pa leaned his forearms on the rough surface of the half wall next to the milking stall. "Your mother is too soft and has spoiled you all your life. You're eighteen—a man now—and you need to start making good decisions. Think about someone besides yourself for a change. This will be your farm one day."

Curt couldn't stand this any longer. He pushed to his feet, wanting the advantage, even if it was only to be had by towering over his father. Why did the man have the power to unsettle him so or stir such a deep anger? "*I am* thinking about someone else. Deborah. She loves me and wants to marry me."

"She's sixteen and has an ailing mother who needs her. If I didn't oversee her farm help, they'd have lost that place when her father died ten years ago."

Curt sucked in a breath, wanting to retaliate, but the response died on his lips. Pa had sacrificed much to keep his own farm going as well as that of the Summers', and never said a word of complaint.

Pa thumped the flat of his hand against the wall.

"Are you going to put aside your foolish notions and settle down to farming so Deborah is guaranteed a good life?"

Curt's spine stiffened. "You know the answer to that. I kill everything I try to grow. I wasn't cut out to herd cattle or plant crops. All I've ever wanted to do is work with wood—to make furniture and create things for people's homes— why can't you respect my choice? Deborah does, and she supports me in it."

"That's all well and good, but is it going to put food on the table? You have no training or experience. It takes years to build a name for yourself before you start making a living."

"I know all that, Pa. You've said it often enough over the years." Curt tried to keep the growl out of his voice. Pa meant well, and Ma would be disappointed in him if he showed disrespect to his father, even if the older man refused to understand. "But I found a man in The Dalles—a master craftsman who's offered to take me on as an apprentice. In four years or so I could open my own shop, or if I'm good enough, he might take me on as a partner. I could do well for myself and Deborah."

Pa shook his head. "Four or five years from now you'll *try* to start your own business. Until then, you'll not make any money. The man will feed you and teach you a craft, but that's all. How can you support a wife and the babies that will follow? Your grandfather tried his hand at furniture making and couldn't make a living." He frowned. "And there's one more thing you've given no thought to."

Curt wondered what could possibly come next. "Yes, sir? And what is that?"

"You don't share the same faith as Deborah. She's lived her whole life with an aim to please God, and you've spent your whole life pleasing yourself."

This time Curt couldn't keep the irritation from his voice. Pa was wading in where he didn't belong. "I attend church with you and Ma."

"That's not what I'm talking about, and you know it. Deborah lives out her faith every day. She cares for her ma, she works at the church, and she loves God with a devotion I've never seen in someone so young.

"You barely tolerate church and have no relationship with God at all. Oil and water don't mix, Curt. Deborah loves you now, but if you continue down the path you've been walking, rebelling against all she holds dear, you'll break her heart and destroy that love. Better you let her go while she's young and still able to find a man who

will care for her—one who believes as she does—
rather than drag her off to a life of poverty without
the strength of a living faith to carry you through
the trials that lay ahead."

"I don't agree." Curt kept his tone even while
pushing down the anger that simmered inside.
"The love we share will overcome anything. She'll
move to The Dalles with me, and we'll be happy
together."

"So you'll force her to choose between you and
her ailing mother instead of settling down and
working her farm?"

"Why does it have to come to that? Maybe her
mother would come with us. Have you thought
about that? Why should Deborah be the one to sac-
rifice everything?"

Pa stared down for several moments then finally
looked up. "Because even at sixteen years of age,
Deborah is the type of woman who will do the right
thing. Her father is buried on that land, and it would
be hard on her ma to leave. You'll destroy Deborah's
respect and love for you if you try to force her to do
otherwise. Listen to me, boy. Don't put her in that
position."

Curt clenched his hands then stuffed them into
his trouser pockets. "I've had enough of this talk. I'm

going to see Deborah."

Pa thumped the palm of his hand against the stall wall. "Don't be foolish, son. If you go off half-cocked and leave the farm, don't come back begging for handouts. You can stay here and work like you ought to, or don't bother returning."

⌘

Five years later—December 1880

Deborah Summers folded a shawl and tried to smooth out the creases, admiring the intricate flowers Sarah Warren had stitched in each corner. She wanted to do the best she could by Jarrod Warren after all he'd done to help them over the years. The poor man had lost his wife yesterday, and he was in no shape to get his house ready for the service tomorrow.

She placed the shawl in Sarah's bureau drawer then lifted her head and met her mother's gaze. "I don't plan to marry, Ma. I don't mean to be disrespectful, but even if a dozen farmers or store owners offer for my hand, I'll stay single."

Her mother sank onto the hand-knitted coverlet draped across the neatly made bed and sighed. "You should have married Timothy Bates, instead of breaking it off a few weeks before you were to wed.

It wasn't fair, Deborah."

Deborah bit her lip to keep from saying something she shouldn't and gave her mother a weak smile.

Ma gripped her shaking hands in her lap and leaned against the ornate headboard. "I'm not long for this world, and I don't want you left alone when I pass. You're twenty-one, my dear, and you need a good man to provide for you. We're not wealthy folks, and I won't leave you much besides a small farm that barely pays its way."

Deborah's brow puckered. She loved her mother but despaired of convincing her she wasn't on her deathbed. "You aren't dying, Ma. I know you've been weak lately, and you lost some weight, but I believe you're getting better."

She plucked a stack of lace-edged kerchiefs from their place on a chair arm and moved them to another bureau drawer, wishing Mr. Warren had given better instructions on where he wanted them to store Sarah's belongings. A trunk lid yawned open against the far wall, and two or three wooden boxes sat empty near the open bedroom door.

Her mother reached out and touched Deborah's arm, bringing her activity to a halt. "I'll never get completely well, Deborah—not after having scarlet fever years ago. You avoided my comment about Timothy Bates, Daughter."

Ma swept a hand around the room. "Even Mr. Warren acknowledges his son isn't coming back. If the death of his own mother didn't draw Curt back to Goldendale, then you need to face the fact he'll never return. It's been five years since he left. You must move on with your life."

Deborah winced, not wanting her mother to see how much her well-meaning words had pierced her heart. She fought against the truth in Ma's comment. Before he'd left, Curt had come to her house and told her he was leaving, that he wasn't good enough for her, but she couldn't accept that then, and wouldn't accept it—not ever.

She knew he loved her and had left because he believed it was right, but it stung, nevertheless. She should have had some say in the matter. How could he walk away and not even stay close enough to visit? Worse yet, he'd only written twice after leaving, and not at all in the past four years.

"You had an excellent chance with Timothy Bates."

Deborah sighed. "I didn't love Timothy, Ma. I never should have agreed to marry him. I was still hurting over Curt, and Timothy's kind words eased some of the pain. But that's not a good reason to marry. I knew he'd be happier with Nadine Garvey. I did him a favor by ending our agreement."

Her mother clucked her tongue. "Be that as it may, it didn't help your future by letting him go. You're a lovely woman now, with plenty of skills that any man would be happy to acquire. But if you wait much longer, you'll be alone the rest of your life."

Deborah shut the drawer a little harder than she'd planned then swung around. "Better to be alone than to marry someone I don't love, while my heart is still tied to another."

"Then untie it, girl. You're being more than a little foolish." Ma flicked a hand at the wardrobe standing open against the far wall. "We'd best get to work and finish this off. I promised Mr. Warren we'd be done before the service tomorrow."

"Not with all the cleaning, too? We can have the front room and kitchen tidied and shining before folks show up, but not the rest of the house. Sarah was ailing for such a long time. I'm afraid Mr. Warren kept up on the farm, but not the house. It's going to take at least a week to set this place back to rights."

"If only I had more energy and strength, we'd get done faster." Ma's voice ended on a weak note, but she pushed to her feet and wobbled across the floor to the walnut wardrobe.

Deborah's heart lurched. Maybe her mother hadn't been exaggerating. "Come sit, and let me do that. There's no need to push yourself."

She wrapped her arm around her mother's shoulders, shocked anew by the sharp bones where there used to be soft flesh. She settled her mother onto the bed again then straightened. "I'll step into Sarah's sitting room and bring a few things in here. We'll need that area somewhat clear before guests arrive, and the easiest course of action is to store things in this room for now."

"Fine, dear. I'll rest, and when I get my breath, I'll help."

"No ma'am. You stay put." Deborah shook her finger and smiled. "That's an order." She headed for the door to the adjoining room, thankful it was close. She'd leave it ajar and listen in case Ma called.

She stepped into the sitting room and stopped, her breath caught in her throat. A man stood with his back toward her. It wasn't Mr. Warren, but something was disturbingly familiar about the set of his shoulders and the fringe of dark brown hair she could see beneath his hat. "Hello? May I help you?"

He pivoted, his hand on the mantle above the

fireplace, and his warm brown eyes captured hers. "Deborah Summers. Well, I'll be. You're the last person I expected to see here."

She dropped the crocheted doilies, her fingers numb and her brain refusing to function. She must be seeing things. It wasn't possible that Curt Warren was standing there, his face wreathed in a nonchalant smile. The shock passed in moments, however, and anger took its place. How dare he return after all these years and act as though nothing had changed! She sank to the floor, blindly groping for the bits of lace, while a storm gathered in the pit of her stomach, ready to erupt.

Chapter 2

Curt held himself steady against the mantle, working hard to stay composed. He wanted to rush across the room and pluck the bits of lace from the floor and present them to the stunning young woman on bended knee. But it had been far too long since he'd seen her, and his tongue was as frozen as his limbs. Couldn't he have come up with something more fascinating than she was the last person he expected to see? She must think him a complete dunderhead—if not worse.

Finally, he pushed himself erect and straightened his jacket, wishing he'd worn his usual everyday clothing and not crammed himself into this suit. But Pa needed to see that he'd attained some measure of success in his chosen career. He held out his hand and smiled. "Let me help you."

She hesitated, and he saw a flicker of what appeared to be anger flash in her eyes, but she finally extended her hand.

"Thank you." Standing, she withdrew and stepped away, putting a wider distance between them.

Curt grimaced at the frown marring Deborah's face. "I came home for Ma's service, but I didn't realize you'd be here. Have I done something wrong?"

"Wrong?" Deborah's frown deepened. "Whatever would give you that idea? It's only been five years since I saw you, and yet you act as though it was last week." She crossed her arms and tossed her head. "Not a single letter in the last four years, even after I told you I'd wait."

Curt's blood thrummed in his ears. "But I told you. . ." He licked his lips. "Did you wait? Are you married? I mean. . ." Warmth rushed into his face at the fury clouding Deborah's expression. "Pardon me. That was rude and disrespectful. As I remember, I told you not to wait—that I wouldn't be back, and you should move on with your life. Dragging you away from your mother wouldn't be fair. I'm sorry if I caused you distress by not continuing to write. I truly thought you understood."

∽

Deborah hunched a shoulder. "It doesn't matter now; and no, I'm not married or betrothed." She lifted her head. "Not that I haven't had offers."

She had no idea why she'd tacked on that last. Maybe due to the flicker of joy she saw in his eyes when she'd said no—a perverse desire to show him she wasn't an old maid with no one who cared to marry her. But she couldn't deny the attraction she still felt for this man, or the longing that had rushed over her when he'd clasped her fingers for those few seconds it had taken her to stand.

She tipped her head toward the next room. "I'm surprised Ma hasn't appeared. I left her resting on the bed, but I'd better check on her."

"Your mother is here, too? I haven't seen Pa yet, so I'm not sure what's going on."

Deborah gave him a slight smile. "I must say I'm quite surprised to see you. You haven't visited since you left." She rested her hand on the doorframe leading into the adjoining room and turned. "Your father asked Ma and me to ready the house for the service and clean out some of your mother's things, but he didn't mention you were coming."

A belated thought struck her, and she sucked in a quick breath. "Curt, I'm so sorry about your ma. She was a good woman, and my mother treasured her friendship."

He nodded, his face grave. "Thank you. Someone from the church sent word, or I wouldn't have known. I wish I could have arrived before she passed." He bowed his head for a moment. "I didn't tell Pa I was coming, so I'm not sure what he'll say when he finds out I'm here."

From listening to Mr. Warren over the past five years, Deborah had a good idea what he might say to his son, but she couldn't destroy Curt's look of tentative hope. "I hope he'll be surprised and happy to see you." She smiled and pushed open the door to the bedroom. "Ma? Are you awake?"

Peeking into the room, she hesitated, then walked softly to the bed, hating to disturb her mother. The older woman lay on the coverlet, eyes closed and hands clasped over her waist. The same pose Deborah had seen her father in, lying in his casket.

Panic gripped her, and she rushed to the bed, certain her mother's words about dying had been prophetic. "Mama?" She touched her mother's cheek, and relief swamped her at the warmth that met her fingertips. "Are you all right?"

She sensed Curt behind her but ignored him, intent on making sure her mother was well. "Wake up, Ma. Someone is here."

"Hmm? Who? What?" Her mother's eyelids fluttered, and she struggled to sit up. She pushed against the headboard and attempted to straighten her skirt. "Oh, my!" Her gaze lifted to just over Deborah's shoulder. "My stars! Is that young Curt Warren, or am I dreaming?"

The bedroom door swung open and thumped against the wall. Deborah and Curt swiveled and stared. Mr. Warren stood in the opening, a scowl marring his otherwise pleasant visage to the extent Deborah barely recognized him.

He pointed at Curt as his bellow filled the room. "What in thunder are you doing here?"

⁓

Curt stiffened, ready to do battle as he'd always done as a young man, then forced his tight muscles to relax. He was no longer the rebellious youth who'd lived in this home. He was a man who'd matured into the kind of person his parents had always hoped for—but somehow he doubted his father would believe that. He could only pray Deborah would, once he had a chance to talk to her alone.

But right now he must deal with the man who stood before him, trembling with anger. Curt held out his hand and stepped forward, forcing a smile he didn't feel. "Pa. It's good to see you, sir."

His father's gaze didn't waver, and his arms stayed at his sides. "I asked you a question. Why are you here?"

Curt flinched at the harsh words. He'd prayed so many times about this reunion. In fact, he'd longed to come home, but his mother's letters had begged him to wait. She'd worked hard to soften his father's attitude, but for some reason Curt couldn't understand, Pa seemed determined to keep him a prodigal for as long as he continued in his chosen career.

"I heard about Ma. She wrote and told me she was sick, but she was certain she was doing better. Then a friend wrote and told me she'd passed." He hung his head and his body shuddered. "I'm sorry, Pa." He raised damp eyes. "I would have been here if I'd known how bad it was."

Pa flicked a hand toward the door. "If you cared, you never would have left in the first place. Maybe you'd best go back to your home. You don't belong in these parts any longer."

Deborah had stood silent beside the bed where her mother sat, but now she moved to stand beside Curt. "Mr. Warren, maybe it would be good to set this aside for the moment. At least until Mrs. Warren is put to rest. Curt didn't have a chance to tell his mother good-bye. Perhaps you could give him a few days before you ask him to leave?"

Pa swung his gaze to Deborah, and Curt saw his hard expression soften, then he heaved a sigh. "All right. I'll do that for you, girl. I appreciate your help here, and yours, Winifred, and I don't want to appear callous or unfeeling at a time when charity should abide in our hearts."

His glare returned to Curt. "You can use your old room and stay—for one week. One week from today, if you decide you want to give up your foolish notions and return to working the farm, we'll talk. Otherwise, you'd best get along home."

Curt winced but gave a slight nod. "Thank you, sir." He had to bite his tongue to keep from saying he'd never push a plow again. There was no sense in riling his father more when he'd opened the door to possible reconciliation—but at what cost? Certainly one Curt would never be able to pay. All he could do now was pray that somehow God would soften his father's heart.

He glanced at Deborah in time to see a flicker of despair cross her face, and he held in a groan. Maybe coming home had been a mistake. All his old feelings for her were returning in a rush, and it appeared he'd opened several old wounds that should have been left closed.

Chapter 3

Deborah clenched her hands in the folds of her skirt and shut her eyes as anxiety turned into relief. Mr. Warren had given in, something she'd prayed the man would do but had not expected. But why hadn't Curt told him he'd stay for good? Surely now that he was back, he'd see how much he was needed. Was there a reason he couldn't do his woodworking here, now that he'd learned a trade?

She longed to throw her arms around him and beg him to heed his father's words—to give them another chance at love and a life together—but fear kept her arms pinned to her sides. His vocation apparently meant more to him than she did, and he'd never seemed to regret what he'd given up for his new life. No matter how much she'd longed for his return, she didn't know if she'd ever be able to trust her life to him again. But was it possible God might be giving them a second chance?

She turned to her mother. "Ma? We should get you home to bed."

Curt touched Deborah's arm. "May I drive you?

Is your buggy in the barn? I can tie my horse to it and ride back."

Deborah's breath caught in her throat as memories returned of past buggy rides. "I don't know, Curt. You should stay here and visit with your father."

Mr. Warren grunted. "I've been without him for five years, I can muddle along for another hour. Besides, Winifred doesn't look well." He shot a hard glance at Curt. "Hitch the buggy and take them home."

Curt nodded, but a mask slipped over his features. "Yes sir." He pivoted and walked out the door without looking back.

Deborah's heart plummeted. Would he be able to tolerate his father for a full week, or would he leave town again right after the service? She'd better guard her emotions and not allow herself to hope.

She placed her arm around her mother's waist, and Mr. Warren moved aside as they crossed the threshold into the other room. "I'll return after I get mother settled, if that's all right? If Curt drives the buggy, I'll ride back with him and work a little longer."

Mr. Warren rushed past them and opened the door. "Please don't worry about it, Deborah." He glanced over his shoulder at the still untidy living area. "I'm sure the neighbors will understand if everything's not perfect."

She shook her head. "Ma just needs to sleep for a bit. If she's worse by the time we get home, I'll stay with her. Otherwise, I'll return."

Her mother waved her hand. "I'm fine. Quit worrying. I'll take a nap and be right as rain in a couple of hours."

Mr. Warren followed them out and helped them into the buggy as Curt held the reins of the restless horse. "Now, Winifred, don't you even think about doing any more work. I won't stand for you making yourself sick on my account. Sarah would have had my hide." Sadness crept across his face, and he choked on the last words.

The drive to their home passed in silence as Curt kept his eyes on the road and Deborah and her mother sat quietly in the seat behind him. Disappointment grew in Deborah as they neared the house and Curt still hadn't spoken. Was he already regretting his decision to spend a few days on his father's farm?

She softly cleared her throat and leaned forward. "If you'll wait, I'd like to get Ma settled then return with you and continue cleaning."

His shoulders tightened, but he gave a brief nod. "Of course."

He pulled the horse to a stop then climbed down and helped them from the buggy. Deborah got her mother in bed, kissed her forehead, and tiptoed out of the room to a still silent Curt. A brief smile flickered then vanished before he handed her up to the front seat, where he sank down beside her. He picked up the reins, released the brake, and urged the horse forward.

Deborah waited, wondering how to broach the subject she longed to know about, and hoping he'd be the one to speak first. Finally, she could stand it no longer. "Curt?"

He turned a warm gaze toward her and smiled.

A soft sigh escaped her lips, and she relaxed. "What was it like there?"

His brows knit together. "You mean in The Dalles? Or at my job?"

"Both. And the man you work for, is he...kind?" She struggled to not pour all her questions out at once, not wanting to overwhelm him, but hoping he'd be willing to talk.

A full grin split his handsome face, and the dimple she'd always loved appeared. "Mr. Colson is one of the finest men I've ever met. He's honest, hardworking, and a true man of God. He doesn't preach at you, but shows you the right way by how he lives.

I've never met a man I respect more."

"More than your father?" As soon as the words left her lips, Deborah wished she could snatch them back again. She knew what a turbulent relationship Curt and his father had maintained throughout Curt's later teen years and how far apart they'd drifted.

Curt's grin faded, and he faced forward again. "Yes. Although I hate to admit that to anyone, I know you understand. You saw how things were between my father and me when I lived at home. It was. . .hard. He was always preaching, always trying to force me to be the person he wanted me to be and never listening to my hopes or dreams."

He pulled back on the reins and drew the horse to a halt, then swiveled to face her. "But now I know it wasn't all his fault. Much of it was mine. I've come to understand how rebellious I was, and how I must have hurt both my parents." He winced. "And you."

She gripped her hands in her lap, barely daring to breathe, hoping he'd continue and she'd hear the words she longed to hear. "So, are you staying this time? Here on the farm with your father?"

His face paled, then flushed. "You know I can't do that. You heard him. The only way he'd accept me is if I give up my trade. I'm no longer an apprentice.

Mr. Colson told me I'm ready to go out on my own now. I can't credit his words, but he says I've exceeded even what he knows, and I could teach others or have my own shop. He's willing to take me on as a partner if I don't care to start my own business, but I haven't decided what's best." He bowed his head for a brief moment then met her gaze. "I want to spend time praying about it first."

⁕

Curt heard Deborah's soft gasp and knew he'd surprised her—possibly even shocked her—with his declaration about prayer. He'd wanted to tell her this entire last year, ever since he'd made the decision to follow in Mr. Colson's footsteps and put God first in his life. He waited, but she still didn't speak. "I thought you might be glad."

The dazed look turned to one of joy. "Oh, but I am! So very glad. I've prayed for this for years. If going away is what it took for you to open your heart to God's love, then I'm glad you did." Her face softened. "But I still don't see why you can't stay here. Your father will come around if you give him time."

"You saw him today. The anger and resentment, demanding I return to farming." He shook his head. "I'll admit, I don't understand. I've *never* understood why he's so against me working with wood. It's a good trade. His own father made furniture for a living."

She shifted beside him, and her arm pressed against his. A jolt shot through him, and he sucked in his breath, surprised that having Deborah near could still affect him. Or had she never stopped affecting him, and he'd simply buried his feelings as deeply as possible to deal with the hurt of having to leave her? He longed to take her in his arms and pour it all out—the full truth of what happened. How his father had insisted he break it off with her, due to her mother's lingering illness and Curt's inability to provide. How he'd come to her home to persuade her to run off with him, only to find her nursing her sick mother and frightened she might die. But he could provide now, and would happily do so, for Deborah, and her mother as well. He'd allowed her to believe he wanted a career and didn't care to remain in Goldendale—and while that was partly true, there had been so much more.

Then his mind returned to the scene in his mother's bedroom with Mrs. Summers today, and the fear he'd seen on Deborah's face as she'd rushed to her. Would it be any more fair now to make Deborah choose between them than it had been when she was sixteen?

She touched his sleeve. "What are you thinking, Curt? What's wrong?" Her imploring eyes probed deep.

He shook his head, not wanting to reveal how much he cared. He picked up the reins. Maybe he should slip away after the service tomorrow and never return. Deborah said she'd had offers, and like five years ago, he couldn't stand the thought of remaining and see her married to some other man. That would destroy him.

⟨∞⟩

The service for Sarah Warren was heavily attended, and with Deborah and Curt's efforts, the parts of the house open to guests shone. Deborah awoke two days later, ready to finish the rest of the Warrens' home, but dreading what she might find when she arrived. Pushing open the door, she slipped inside, praying Curt wouldn't be gone.

A cheery whistle emanated from the kitchen and relief weakened her muscles. She'd know Curt's whistle anywhere. She tapped on the doorframe, waited a second, then stepped into the kitchen as he swung around. A smile brightened his countenance. "You're up early. There's no need for you to keep cleaning the house. I'm sure you have plenty of work to do at home, with your mother not well."

Deborah's smile faded as the realization struck her that Curt apparently wasn't as pleased to see her as she'd hoped. She moved into the room, her chin high, and reached for a towel lying beside the stack of wet dishes. "I see you've learned how to tackle a few household chores, but this is my job, not yours. Your father has been a blessing to me and Ma since Pa died, and I see this as a way to pay back a small part of our debt. Ma is stronger today, and she's doing a few of the inside chores and leaving the supper preparations to me."

"Ah, I see. All right, then. Let's have at it together." Curt plucked the towel out of her hand and tossed it on the countertop with an impish glance. "Those will dry fine on their own. What else is on your list of things that must be done? Sorting clothing again, or something else?"

"Boxes, I think. There are several crates in the attic your father wants me to go through, to see if there's anything worth saving. He believes most of them are full of old clothing or yardage your mother saved that might be ruined by now, but he asked that I check."

Curt nodded. "I'll get a pry bar to remove the nails. Once all the lids are off, I might run out to the barn to clean my horse's stall, then tote anything downstairs you've decided needs to be moved. Will that work?"

Joy bubbled inside that he wanted to help—better yet, that he planned to spend time alone with her. Other than the ride back to his farm, she'd had only snatches of time without his father or her mother or a helpful neighbor stopping by. "Yes, thank you. I'd like that." She tried to keep the eagerness out of her voice, but something in his answering glance told her she might not have succeeded.

They climbed the stairs to the attic, and Curt pushed open the narrow door at the top of the steps. "Whew." He waved his hand in front of his nose. "It's not too pleasant up here. Want me to bring a few boxes downstairs to work where the air is fresher?" He looked around the cramped space. "You'll have better light, as well."

She shrugged, not anxious to return to the living area where some well-meaning person might drop by and interrupt whatever conversation could develop. "Let's stay here for a bit. Maybe open a few boxes and see if they look like something I need to sort through. If most of them are musty old clothing, you can take those down."

"Fair enough." He dragged a wooden crate from a dark corner and rolled up his sleeves. "I'm glad you wore a full apron. It's pretty dusty up here." Sticking the edge of a bar under the lip of the crate, he pressed down, the muscles in his forearms bulging.

Deborah tried not to stare, but couldn't quite help herself. He'd changed so much since she saw him five years ago. He'd gone away a boy of eighteen and returned as a mature man. One who had made his way in the world and knew what he wanted from life—and one who had learned to turn to the Lord during times of indecision and trial. The kind of man she'd always hoped he would become.

He glanced up, the final nail screeching as it reluctantly released its hold. "That's the last one. Looks like you were right, this one is full of clothes." He moved to the next and repeated the process. "Yard goods? Ma loved to sew. I'm guessing we'll find several of these boxes. If any of the cloth is still good, the church ladies might want it for sewing projects."

Deborah nodded and set about digging to the bottom of the crate he'd pried open, sneezing from the dust as she did so. "They'll have to be laundered and checked for holes, but some of this is still good."

He sat back on his haunches. "Want me to tote them downstairs? Or open a few others first?"

She gazed around and spotted a stack in another corner, then noticed a lone box pushed under the eaves. "If you don't mind opening that one first, then a couple of those others, I'll have plenty to do until you return."

He nodded and set to work, pausing occasionally to wipe perspiration from his forehead. "All right, looks like that's it. I'll take a couple of these with me. I won't be gone long."

She watched him cross the room, carrying the heavy load as though it were feather pillows. "I'll be here."

A warm chuckle drifted from the top of the staircase, and she thought she heard him say "I'm glad," as his steps echoed on the hard wood, but she couldn't be sure.

She moved to the crate that had been off to one side, her mind wandering to what might have been if Curt hadn't left town. Would they be married and living in their own home, with possibly a baby or two? If only he could reconcile with his father and find a way to stay.

Removing the loosened lid from the crate, she glanced inside, certain she'd see more clothing or sewing goods. A variety of odd-shaped objects wrapped in cloth surprised her instead. She touched the linen, only to note its fragility. How long had this been stored, and did Curt have any idea what it might be? She hesitated, wondering if she should unwrap the objects. But Mr. Warren had been firm. Go through the boxes and determine what should stay and what should be donated or thrown.

She plucked out a long object and carefully unwrapped it. Her breath caught, and she stared at an exquisite hand-carved statue of a woman, clothed in a robe and sandals, her face alight with joy. Hurriedly, Deborah removed the remaining objects and placed them reverently on the floor around her. A beautiful nativity scene stood revealed, complete with a manger, cows and sheep; wise men and shepherds; along with the most lifelike depiction she'd ever seen of the baby Jesus and his family. Amazing. From the condition of the cloth, the pieces had to have been wrapped decades ago, and it was obvious they'd not been touched in years.

Boots clomped up the final few steps, and she raised her head. "Curt?" As soon as he appeared through the door, she waved him over. "Do you know where these came from?"

Chapter 4

Curt stared at Deborah sitting on the dusty floor, her skirt flared around her and the beautifully carved pieces of wood standing just beyond. He knelt beside her, barely daring to breathe. "What in the world?" He gently cradled the figure of baby Jesus lying in a manger and stroked the wood with his fingertip. "These are exquisite. I've never seen such fine detail. These were in that box?"

She nodded, a frown puckering her lovely face. "Yes. I assume you didn't carve them, as the cloth protecting them is so old. Your grandfather was a woodworker, correct? Do you suppose they were his?"

Curt examined each piece before he replied then set the last wise man reverently on the floor. "Very possible, although I don't see why Ma wouldn't have brought these out each Christmas. What do you want to do with them?"

Deborah brightened, her blue eyes sparkling. "I'd love to take them downstairs and put them on the mantle for Christmas. It's only two weeks away. Do you think your father would mind?"

"I can't imagine why he would. I'll move them for you. Do you want to do more today?" He glanced around, taking in the small pile of boxes not yet sorted and the streaks of dirt smudging Deborah's face. "Or have you had quite enough of the dirt and stale air by now?"

She giggled. "I must look a sight. But you aren't a lot better yourself." She pointed to his head, where a hat usually resided. "It looks like you're trying a new hairstyle, with little points all over the place."

He slapped his hand to his hair and groaned. "I guess if we still care after seeing each other at our worst then. . ." He snapped his lips closed, horrified at what he'd almost said, and shocked that he'd truly meant it. Where was he headed with that kind of statement? Was he ready to declare himself and choose to stay in Goldendale?

No. As much as he cared for Deborah, he needed to think this through. He must pray before he dove into anything. There was no room for regrets in his life, and he certainly didn't want Deborah to have to deal with the sorrow of a hastily made decision. He'd experienced enough of that as a youth.

"I'm sorry. Please forgive me for speaking out of turn."

She hunched one shoulder and turned her head.

"I knew you were teasing. It's all right."

But it wasn't all right. He'd seen the disappointment reflected on her face and watched the joy drain from her eyes before she'd turned away. If only he could find a way to reconcile with his father, or move back to The Dalles and marry Deborah without taking her mother from her home.

"Here. I'll help you pack these and take them to the parlor. In fact, if you want to go clear the mantle, I'll be a few minutes behind you, then you can set these out. We can even find fir boughs to tuck around them if you'd like." He kept his voice light, hoping her smile would return—praying he hadn't hurt her too deeply—again.

A few minutes later he arrived in the cozy parlor that his mother had loved so much. Deborah had removed the old clock from the wide oak mantle and readied it for the holy family that would reside there.

He breathed easier, loving Deborah's excitement as she clasped her hands in front of her waist and rocked back and forth from her tiptoes to her heels. "I'll set the crate on the chair where you can easily reach it. I need to make one more trip to the barn. Do you want me to wait and help you set up the figures?"

She shook her head. "No, thank you. I'd love to do it, if you don't mind. Then you can tell me what you think when you return and help me move them if they need it."

He nodded then stepped forward, unable to resist any longer. As he drew close, she froze, staring up at him with an expectant expression. He lifted a finger and tucked a loose curl behind her ear, then stroked her cheek. "I do care, Deborah. I wasn't teasing upstairs. I simply don't know how to make it all work, but I care. Can you accept that much for now?"

She looked at him, her eyes brimming with tears. "Yes. I think so. But I'm afraid."

"I'll talk to you first if I decide to leave. I promise."

She wiped her damp cheek and stepped away. "But you won't promise not to leave?"

He hesitated, not sure how to reply. His heart longed to promise he'd stay forever—that he'd never leave her again—but could he keep that promise and not take her away from the mother she needed to care for? It all came back to the problem of five years ago. His father wouldn't tolerate him living in this house or being part of his life if he didn't take up farming, and Curt couldn't imagine abandoning his woodworking.

"I'll promise to do my best to find a way to make this work. I promise to pray, and I ask that you do the same. Can that be enough for today?"

She gave a silent nod then smiled. "It can. Now, let me get busy." She waved him toward the door. "You do what you need to do, and let me rejoice in the beauty of this nativity."

❧

Curt rushed through the chores he'd put off too long, knowing it would be one more strike against him if his father noticed they weren't done on time. He longed to return to the woman who'd captured his heart at a deeper level than he'd thought possible. He realized now he hadn't really loved her as a wayward, eighteen-year-old boy—not in the way she deserved to be loved. He had been too selfish, too thoughtless at the time. But what was he now, if he couldn't set aside his own desires and show her true love?

He hurried to the house, wanting to see her again, praying they could find a way to sort through this dilemma. Pushing open the front door, he stepped inside then closed it and drew a deep breath. He strode through the entry and stopped just inside the parlor door in time to see his father raise a fist in the air and shake it.

The older man's bellow filled the room. "What is going on here? Where did you get those?"

Deborah stood pressed against the wall next to the fireplace, bewilderment covering her face. Curt strode across the room and stopped by her side. He took her hand in his and turned to confront his red-faced father. "Quit shouting, Pa. You're scaring her. You can do that with me, but not Deborah."

The red didn't fade from his father's face, and his entire body shook, but the force of his words diminished a little. "I asked you a question, and I demand an answer. Where did those come from, and why have you put them on my mantle?"

Deborah squeezed Curt's hand then released it. "I found them in the attic while sorting through boxes, sir. I assumed they were a family heirloom that you'd forgotten about and that you might enjoy displaying them. I apologize for not asking you first."

The tension seemed to ease from his father's stiff frame as a shudder ran through him. "I don't want them there. Pack them back in the box and put them in the attic. Or take them out to the refuse pile for all I care. I never want to see them again."

Curt placed his hand on Deborah's shoulder as she moved toward the mantle. "Wait, please." He leveled a hard gaze on his father. "What's going on here? I'm not tossing this work of art. Where did it come from? Was it grandfather's?"

Color started to build in the older man's face again, and he swiveled and headed for the door. "Don't ask questions about what doesn't concern you." He stormed out of the room, and the front door slammed so hard the pieces on the mantle shivered.

Deborah sank into the nearest chair and put her hands over her face. "What have I done? Your father must hate me for touching something I shouldn't have."

Curt knelt beside her and cradled one of her hands in his own. "Look at me, dearest." He waited until she complied. "This is not your fault. You followed his instructions by going through the boxes, so you did nothing wrong. I'll help box them up and take you home. There's no need for you to do any more today. Or ever, for that matter. If you choose not to return, no one will blame you."

She burrowed her hand deeper inside his. "I'm truly not afraid of your father; he just startled me. I thought he'd be pleased, especially if I'd found something his father made. I wish I knew what was wrong and how to help."

Curt shook his head. "I've wondered most of my life about why he despises my grandfather's wood-working. I've never understood, and he won't talk about it. Don't worry yourself. It's his problem, not yours."

"But he's your father, Curt. We need to care about what's worrying him."

"I know, dear, but I've tried, and it's never done any good." He released her hand and smiled. "Now will you let me take you home?"

"I don't think so. We'll take these up to the attic, then I want to finish the boxes you uncovered." She gave him a warm smile. "Truly, I'm fine, and when I go home, I can drive myself. Your father has been so kind to Ma and me over the years. He's allowed one outburst when something is bothering him."

Curt stood and moved to the mantle. "How about we pack these, and then I'll take them up while you work on something else downstairs?"

"All right, thank you."

They finished in a companionable silence, then Curt toted the crate to the attic. He tacked the lid on then perched on the hard surface, his chin propped on his hands. That scene with his father had shaken him more than he'd realized. He'd been especially disturbed by the shock on Deborah's face. There was no way he could return to The Dalles and leave her behind.

He knew that now. He loved her more than his passion for woodworking. Maybe it was time to declare himself and do his best to mend fences with Papa, even if that meant returning to farm work and building furniture on the side. Surely he could work something out to satisfy them both.

He lunged to his feet as relief flooded through him, then took the stairs as fast as he could, eager to share his decision with Deborah and see if she'd be willing to be his wife. He didn't want to startle her, so he slowed his pace and walked quietly toward the living room, pausing when he heard his father's voice. It was quieter than last time, but Curt wasn't about to allow the man to bully Deborah or chastise her again. He reached the open doorway and paused, wanting to understand what he might be dealing with before bursting in.

He leaned closer to better hear his father.

"I'm sorry for my behavior, Deborah. It was unkind of me to take my anger out on you. I hope you'll forgive me."

Curt heaved a sigh and relaxed. He didn't want to walk in and embarrass his father when he'd humbled himself to this degree. Better to wait till

Deborah accepted the apology and the conversation moved to something new.

Deborah's soft voice barely reached his ears. "It's all right, Mr. Warren, truly. I'm so sorry my actions caused you pain, but neither Curt nor I knew the nativity would do so. It's a lovely piece, one I'd be proud to call my own. I would never have brought it out if I'd known you didn't care to see it displayed."

The older man harrumphed then cleared his throat. "Speaking of Curt, there's something I feel I must say, if you're willing to listen."

There was no response, and Curt assumed she must have given silent assent, as he heard his father rush on.

"I'm afraid you're going to get your heart broken again. The boy isn't stable. He has no intention of staying here. He values the new life he's built and plans to leave again. I hope you'll guard yourself against getting involved, and focus on your mother."

Curt waited several long moments for Deborah to reply, praying she'd spurn his father's declaration and declare her own feelings for him. Finally, he heard a rustle of her skirts, and he leaned closer to hear her reply.

"I see. Thank you for sharing your concerns."

Another moment passed with nothing further,

and Curt's stomach twisted into a knot. She must no longer trust him. She believed his father's assessment of his character and chose to listen to him rather than take a chance on loving Curt. Not that he blamed her. He'd brought this on himself by leaving the first time and not keeping in touch. He backed away from the doorway as carefully as he could and left the house, his heart too sore to listen further.

Chapter 5

Deborah thought long and hard about what her answer should be to Curt's father—a man she'd come to respect and care for over the years since her own father had died. She didn't want to reject his declaration outright, but she didn't believe he understood his son or had noted how much he'd changed. She gripped her hands in her lap and worked to compose herself then lifted her eyes to his.

"I'm sorry you feel that way, Mr. Warren. I know Curt disappointed and hurt you when he left the first time, but I believe he's a changed man. I can't say for sure he won't leave again, but if he does, I believe it will be because he's prayed and thinks it's the right thing to do. He promised he'll talk with me before he makes a final decision, and I trust him. I wish you could open your heart and see the man he's become."

"Humph." Mr. Warren jerked upright from his stance against the wall. "Then he has you fooled, the same way he fooled his mother. She always believed he'd come home one day a changed man, serving the Lord and willing to settle down, but he never did. The boy never had any real faith of his own. He wanted his own way and wasn't willing to pray about anything. What makes you think he will now?"

"Because he told me." Deborah bit her lip, not willing to share that Mr. Colson had been more of a fatherly influence on Curt's life than the man standing before her. But she must tell him something. "He said that circumstances and people where he lives now had opened his eyes to the truth of the gospel—that he sees what his immaturity cost others and how he'd lived a selfish life. He's changed, Mr. Warren. Curt's made a true commitment, and I believe he'll walk it out."

"I hope you're right, but I hoped that before and nothing came of it." His voice was gruff, and he shook his head. "I'll try to keep an open mind, though, and not be so quick to judge. I thank you for telling me. I just wish he'd done so himself."

Deborah rose to her feet and stepped close, placing her hand on his arm. "I think he's afraid to, sir—afraid that you might reject him again."

The man reared back as though he'd been burned. "I love my boy. That's a foolish thing for him to think or say. Besides, he left, not me. He's the one who needs to apologize and make things right. I'll forgive him if he does that, but it's on his shoulders, not mine."

He pivoted and walked away, his body stiff and unyielding.

Deborah sighed and shook her head. Mr. Warren hadn't changed as much as she'd hoped. Now she'd better pray his obstinate attitude didn't discourage Curt to the point he'd fulfill his father's dire prediction.

∞

The next day, Curt finished the morning chores in the barn. He'd done the milking before breakfast and returned now to clean out the stalls. The one thing he enjoyed about farm work was milking— there was something soothing about the repetitive action and the mesmerizing splash of the milk in the pail.

He was at a total loss as to what to do next. His father had made it clear he didn't want or need his help in the fields or with the few cows he owned, and there was little else to do in this farming community.

If only he had his woodworking tools. Even more than that, he wished Deborah would welcome his presence as she finished sorting his mother's personal items. But he'd determined to give her time—to not press her for a day or two. After the conversation he overheard, he feared she'd lost hope that he'd ever really change.

He pitched a forkful of dirty straw into a pile and wiped his sleeve across his forehead. He couldn't blame her, since he'd not contacted her in the last four years. It had been too hard, knowing things could never work out between them, and that she'd probably be married to someone else soon. A friend in Goldendale had written him, letting him know that more than one young man was interested in Deborah, and then wrote again, telling him when she'd gotten engaged. That almost killed him—he was sick for a week and had produced the worst work of his life.

He rested his chin on the handle of the pitchfork. This uncertainty was even worse. When he'd seen her that first day after he'd returned and realized she wasn't married, hope had returned. Now it came close to withering again, and despair gripped him in talons so tight he could barely breathe. Maybe he'd stay in the barn all day until she was gone.

The crunch of buggy wheels on the pebbles outside drew him to a large chink in the wood. Deborah climbed down from the seat and walked to the horse's head. She'd want to unhitch and turn the horse into a stall. Time to quit being a coward. He swung open the door as she reached it and mustered what he hoped would pass as a pleasant look, but he couldn't manage a smile. "Good morning. I'll unhitch for you if you want to get started inside."

Her brows drew together, and she stared up at him. "Is your father upset again?"

He groaned inwardly. She'd always been too good at reading him, but he didn't see the slightest flicker of personal interest beyond worry about his father. "No, he's fine."

She drew the horse forward into the alley between the stalls but didn't reply.

He extended a hand. "There's no need for you to get your skirts dirty."

She hesitated, then sniffed. "Fine. If you don't care to talk about it, I'll get to work." The barn door creaked again as she let herself out, but Curt didn't stir. It hurt too much to see the woman he loved walking away from him. Now he understood a tiny bit what she must have felt all those years ago, when he left Goldendale and didn't return.

❧

Deborah flounced out of the barn but slowed her pace halfway to the house, her steps beginning to drag. It was obvious something was bothering Curt, but he didn't appear interested in telling her what it might be. That irritated her even more than his cool reply. When they were young and in love, he'd told her everything—except for how much he must have hated farming. She'd known he chafed at the chores and longed to work with wood for a living, but she'd never truly believed he'd strike off on his own and leave the farm and his father—and her—behind.

She hadn't believed it even when he'd come to the house that horrible day and said he was leaving to apprentice in The Dalles, Oregon. Deep inside, she'd known he'd last a few weeks or months at most and come home to her. But his letters had stopped completely that first year, and her hope had begun to fade.

Her chin lifted then she marched the rest of the way to the house. Maybe she should have married when she'd had the chance.

Her pace slowed—was that fair? Curt could have had a bad morning with his father again and didn't want her to worry. Surely that was the case. Once he finished stabling the mare, he'd come in and help her, as he had the past few days.

She wished she could decorate the house for Christmas. It seemed such a shame that Mr. Warren wouldn't allow her to display the lovely nativity set. Fir and pine abounded in the region. Her lips curved at a new thought. Maybe Curt would take her in the sleigh to gather some if the snow arrived soon. They'd had several flurries, but it hadn't stayed long, which was certainly not typical for this time of year.

She slipped into the house, wondering if Mr. Warren was around or out in the fields. Drawing off her heavy coat, she headed for Sarah Warren's private room, wanting to finish the last few drawers and a trunk that she had yet to open. Sometimes she felt funny about going through another woman's personal things, but it seemed neither Mr. Warren nor Curt cared to tackle the tasks.

The flat-topped trunk sat under the window. A cream-colored cloth with delicate, hand-stitched embroidery in each corner covered most of the top, with a piece of cut glass perched in the center. Sarah fingered the lovely bowl, then set it aside and removed the cover.

She lifted her head and listened, wondering when Curt would come in, then she shoved the thought aside. If he didn't care to spend time with her, she certainly didn't plan to pursue him.

The lid opened with a slight squeak, as though the hinges hadn't been worked in years. She lifted out a tray with shallow, open compartments after giving it a quick glance. It appeared to be mostly sewing supplies that she could sort later. More sewing goods lay beneath, along with a stack of books.

Deborah plucked out the top three and set them aside. The next book caught her attention, as did three more identical ones beneath—all cloth-bound volumes that showed little sign of wear, the corners still crisp, and the dark brown color not dimmed by exposure to light.

She looked at the spine of the one on top and drew in a breath. It appeared to be a journal or diary of some sort, as did the rest. Was she trespassing on Mr. Warren's property again? Her hands trembled as she considered whether to ask him first, or place it back inside and shut the lid. But he'd told her only to avoid his room and the desk in the living area— he'd been very explicit that all the items in his wife's rooms were to be thoroughly examined, as she didn't feel up to doing so.

The first page was dated December 26, but there was no indication of ownership. Perhaps if she read a page or two, she might get a sense of whom it belonged to. She supposed it must be Sarah Warren's, although without an identifying year, it could belong to a parent or grandparent. She read the first page with interest, intrigued by the sweeping script and conversational style.

> *I'm so worried about Jarrod—I wish he would talk to me. Something is wrong, but he won't say what it is. He gave me a lovely gift yesterday, a cut-glass bowl that I plan to keep in my room where I can see it as soon as I awaken. But he's been glum and unresponsive. Not that he didn't show enthusiasm over the shirt I made for him, but he turned aside with very little comment over the whittling knife that I was certain he'd love. I must try to find out what the matter is when he visits again tomorrow.*

Deborah turned the page, wondering if it was right to read more, but unable to resist the story for long. The second page was dated December 28. Had Sarah had a busy day and been unable to write the day before?

> *Jarrod came to visit last night so we could talk about wedding plans, but I had a hard time breaking through his silence. Finally, before he left, he went out to his buggy and returned with a crate, which he shoved into my arms. I asked if it was another Christmas gift and assured him*

he'd already given me enough. He gave a harsh laugh and shook his head. "Not a gift that was meant for you in the beginning, but if you don't take it, I'll destroy it."

I peeked inside the cloth wrappings and was amazed at what met my gaze. A beautiful carved nativity, each piece intricate. I had withdrawn three when he grabbed one, the figure of a shepherd, and drew back his arm as though he planned to throw it. I stopped him in time and demanded he explain.

"I made it for my father for Christmas," he said. "When he saw it, all he could do was criticize. It was no good. I would never be able to make a living from this type of work. He said he had struggled to provide for our family all these years, and I'd do the same, only worse, since I had no talent to speak of. I never want to see them again. Take them and put them away where I can't find them, or I'll burn them."

I saw that he meant it, and I wrapped up the wonderful creations and took the crate to my room. There was no use trying to dissuade him. I will try to broach the subject again in a few days.

Deborah's hand shook as she turned the page,

knowing that she was unlocking the key to Mr. Warren's anger at her discovery of the nativity set in the attic. Would Sarah say any more about it, or was this where the matter was left? The following page shed very little light on the subject.

December 31. I tried talking to Jarrod again tonight about his gift to his father, hoping he might attempt once more to give it to Mr. Warren, but he turned away in obvious pain. I assured him the pieces were magnificent, but he only scoffed. His father is considered one of the best woodworkers in the valley, and he should know whether Jarrod has talent or not. His father had only been able to eke out a living with his woodworking and must farm on the side to get by, so Jarrod believes that farming is the more sensible career.

I told him not to give up on his carving, but he said he'd stored his tools and will never touch them again. His father's words cut deep. The man might have meant well, trying to save his son the pain of being a poor provider, but I fear he's wounded my love's spirit to the point where he might never recover.

More than anything, I want Jarrod to reconcile

*with his father. I fear that if he doesn't, he'll carry
his hurt and bitterness into our marriage and pass
it along to any children we might have. I pray that
somehow God heals his heart and brings him to a
place of peace, before it's too late.*

Deborah picked up another journal from the
bottom of the pile and glanced at the first page, noting it was penned only a few months before Sarah's death. She turned to the last page and sucked
in a quick breath as her eyes caught Curt's name.
She read the final paragraph then closed the book,
suddenly ashamed of reading such a personal entry. Should she give the diaries to Curt, so he could
see his father through his mother's eyes? Or would
he be angry at her because she'd read his mother's
private thoughts and turn away from her in disgust? She'd put this back where she found it for now
and spend a day or two praying before she decided.
Maybe God would help her find a way to reconcile
the two men before Curt's week was up.

Chapter 6

Curt wished he'd driven over to get Deborah in his buggy so he could offer to drive her home later. The snow was falling and the wind had picked up, but that wasn't what had stopped him. He'd do it if he thought she'd care to have his company, but after what his father had said to her, he doubted that was the case.

He finished harnessing Deborah's horse, knowing she'd be leaving soon. It had taken all his will-power to stay away from the part of the house where she was working today.

He sucked in a breath and patted the mare's neck then strode to the house. He'd see what her attitude toward him might be, then take it from there. Swinging open the door, he almost collided with Deborah. Her words were stiff as he glimpsed her solemn expression. "I apologize. I'll slow down and watch where I'm going next time." No smile warmed her features; no light shone in her eyes.

"I'll drive you home, if you'd like. I can keep the buggy and drive over to get you in the morning."

She shook her head, her dark curls dancing under her bonnet. She buttoned the neck of her heavy coat as she moved past him, not meeting his eyes. "I've driven that short section of road hundreds of times without you, Curt. There's no reason for you to come out in the cold."

"I don't mind." He bit his tongue before he blurted out how much he longed to spend time with her—how much he'd missed her company today and regretted not offering to help. If only she'd say something to let him know how she felt.

"Thank you, but no. I don't care to be without a conveyance, in case Ma needs a doctor. Besides, if the snow moves in and gets deep, I'll probably stay home tomorrow." Sadness flickered over her face as she glanced at him.

He scrambled to think of something to say but couldn't come up with a thing. Had she believed Pa that he planned to leave? Didn't she trust him after he'd told her he'd discuss his plans with her, if he made the decision to return to The Dalles?

Curt stepped aside. "As you wish. But if you'd like to come tomorrow, I'll hitch the sleigh and pick you up—if there's enough snow."

Her eyes lit with something akin to expectation, then after several seconds she looked away. "I do have a few things to finish, so that would be nice. I'd better hurry on home now and fix supper before Ma starts to worry."

"How is she?" Curt walked beside her to the barn and tugged open the door, anxious to get them both out of the wind.

"A little better. I'm not so worried about leaving her now. I'm being cautious about wanting a buggy close by, but I don't think she'll take a turn for the worse."

They continued in silence, and Curt shoved down the hope trying to bubble to the surface. Just because Mrs. Summers was better now didn't mean it would last. The poor woman had struggled with health issues for years, and Curt well remembered Deborah's fear when they were young that she'd lose her mother soon.

He helped her into the buggy and held her hand a few moments longer than necessary. "Deborah?"

She settled onto the seat and released his hand to pick up the reins. "Yes?" The word had a breathless aspect.

"Is everything. . .all right? Is there anything you'd like to tell me?"

"That *I'd* like to tell *you*?" She shook her head. "No. Should there be?"

"I suppose not." He hesitated a moment, then rushed on, still praying she'd show some indication of her feelings. "Well, I won't keep you. The wind will cut through your warm clothing, so you'd better hurry." He kept his voice neutral, not wanting to press her, but wishing she'd feel safe to confide her fears.

She averted her head and stared between the horse's ears. "Yes, you're right." She shook the reins and clucked to the mare. "Get along there. It's time we got home."

Curt stared after the departing buggy, praying he could find a way to make things right.

∽∾∿

Deborah looked out the window at dawn, hoping for enough snow that Curt would come for her in the sleigh. Unfortunately, the wind had blown the storm somewhere else before it had a chance to drop more than an inch or two. Her horse would have no problem drawing the buggy, and the runners on the sleigh would scrape and bump over the ruts and rocks in the road.

Two hours later, with her mother fed, the kitchen clean, and a pot of stew simmering on the stove for dinner, Deborah pulled her horse to a stop in front of the Warren home. She waited for Curt's cheerful whistle but didn't hear it, so she climbed down and tied the mare to the hitching rail. The wind had calmed, and the horse would be fine while she saw if anyone was home.

She knocked on the door, not expecting anyone to answer, and was startled when it swung open and Mr. Warren stood inside.

His face crinkled in a welcoming smile. "Deborah. Come in out of the cold. I didn't expect you today. You've done so much already. I assumed you'd take a day or two to get caught up at home."

"Is Curt here?" She wished she could retract her words as the smile on the older man's face dimmed.

"I sent him to town to get a few supplies. He should be back in an hour or two, although I don't expect he'll be around much longer. He's getting itchy feet, I can tell. Just you wait and see, he'll disappear soon." He wagged his head then took her coat as she slipped out of it.

Deborah drew in a quick breath. "Mr. Warren? Would you have a minute to talk?"

He wrinkled his forehead, but nodded. "It's always a pleasure to visit with you, Deborah. I have a pot of coffee on. Come into the kitchen and sit."

They settled down at the table with their mugs. Fragrant steam rose, making Deborah's mouth water.

She almost decided not to broach the subject of his wife's journal, in the hope of continuing this genial atmosphere, but forced herself to press on. "I found some things while sorting items in Mrs. Warren's trunk that I wanted to ask you about."

Pain washed Mr. Warren's features, and then he nodded. "Go ahead."

She bit her lip then plunged forward. "It's a set of journals."

He brightened, and a smile curved his mouth. "Ah, yes. Sarah was always one to write down her thoughts. Someday I'll read her journals. But I thought she'd given me all of them for safekeeping. You say you found more?"

"Yes. In the trunk in her room. They didn't have her name on them, and I wasn't sure who they belonged to or what I should do with them." Sudden panic assailed her as she realized she'd have to admit she'd read a few pages. "I'm so sorry. I fear I've overstepped again. I read parts of them, as I thought it might be from an older relative. I got so caught up in her wonderful narrative that I'd read more than I planned before I realized. I do hope you'll forgive me."

He grinned. "My girl could tell a story, that's for sure. I don't mind you reading it, as long as it wasn't too personal."

"Well. . ." She winced and averted her gaze. "It was personal. She shared how proud she was of your talent. Then, on the last page, years later, she talked about Curt and his love for the same craft—carving and working with wood. She was so sad—she longed for the two of you to reconcile. . ." She sucked in a deep breath then rushed on. "She talked about the nativity you made for your father."

Mr. Warren's expression turned to granite, his hands so tight around his mug it looked like he might crush it. "I don't want to talk about that."

Deborah couldn't help herself. "But I care for you and Curt, Mr. Warren. I understand your wife's pain and longing for the two of you to reconcile. He's following in his grandfather's footsteps, but they're your footsteps as well. Curt longs for your approval and acceptance. Please think about it, for his mother's sake, if not for mine." She pushed up from her chair. "I think I'll go home now. I've imposed enough. If you still want me to come tomorrow, I'll finish up then."

He gave a bare nod, his lips pressed in a tight line. "Tomorrow is fine."

"I'll see myself out." She moved with heavy tread to the door, wondering yet again if she'd done the right thing. Mr. Warren had only recently lost his wife, but if something didn't change soon, he'd lose his son, as well.

∞

Curt dragged himself out of bed the next morning. Deborah had seemed so preoccupied and distant of late. Pa hadn't come in the house the entire evening last night, but stayed in the barn until long after bedtime. Could his father be so disgruntled with him that he didn't care to even be in the same house?

It was time to return to The Dalles, even though his heart longed to remain here. Swiftly, he packed his saddlebags with his few clothes and personal items and headed to the kitchen. He found a paper and pencil and scribbled a note for his father, on the chance he might not see him before he left. This time he wouldn't disappear and not return—but he had to talk to Mr. Colson and explain that he needed more time to decide a course of action. He wanted to marry Deborah, but it might take weeks, if not months, to regain her trust.

He'd ride to her farm and say good-bye—he'd given his word not to leave again without telling her. Slinging the saddlebags over his shoulder, he headed outside. There was no point in delaying this. Hopefully Pa would come in from feeding the cows in the pasture, but if he didn't, he'd find the note and know his son would return. It should only take him a few days to ride to The Dalles and back, as long as a snowstorm didn't dump too much snow to make the return trip.

His stomach churned, and he swallowed hard, not wanting to give way to grief. What if Deborah would never accept his suit or learn to trust him? It didn't matter. He'd wait the rest of his life if that's what it took, and put up with whatever his father saw fit to dish out, for as long as the man continued to live. If only he and Pa could repair their relationship. He grunted. Not that there was much to repair. They'd been close years ago, before he'd decided he didn't want to farm and turned to woodworking instead.

He saddled his horse and slung the bags over its rump then secured them with leather straps. The air had a harsh bite to it, and he buttoned up his coat and tucked the woolen scarf that Deborah had given him so many years ago around his neck.

The front door of the house banged, and Curt's head whipped up. Pa must be back. But why hadn't he come to the barn first? He waited, wondering if he should go inside or wait for Pa to read the note and come see if he'd gone. He swung into the saddle, his decision made. If Pa wanted to talk, he'd come out. If he didn't show up in the next minute or two, he'd ride for Deborah's farm.

The barn door crashed open and Pa stood silhouetted in the dim light of the winter morning. He strode forward and grabbed the horse's reins. "What do you think you're doing? What's wrong with you, boy? Get off that horse. I've got something to say."

Chapter 7

Deborah drew up in front of Mr. Warren's house and swiveled toward her mother, happy Ma felt strong enough to come. She turned toward the barn. Was that Mr. Warren she heard bellowing at the top of his voice? What in the world could be the matter? She prayed he wasn't injured or sick and calling for help. She plucked up her skirts to keep them from dragging in the mud and rushed toward the open door.

"Deborah! That you?" Mr. Warren's voice boomed from the interior. "Come in here."

Hands shaking, Deborah turned to her mother. "Will you be all right if I run in for a minute, or would you like to come?"

Ma smiled. "From the sound of things, you might need some support. I'll stay inside the door in case I'm not wanted, but I'd like to come."

Deborah tied the horse to the rail and helped her mother down, then hurried inside. She waited for her eyes to adjust then spotted Curt standing beside his saddled horse, and Mr. Warren all aquiver beside him. She left her mother by the door and walked forward. "I'm here. Is something wrong?"

Mr. Warren beckoned to her, and as she drew near, he took her hand, giving it a light squeeze. "Do you love this son of mine?"

She gasped and felt the blood drain from her face. "Mr. Warren! What kind of question is that?"

He swiveled to Curt. "You've been mooning over Deborah every day since you got home, but now you're going to ride off and leave again. What's wrong with you, boy?"

Curt stared at his father, seemingly unable to find a reply. His gaze shifted to Deborah and stark longing blazed from his eyes.

Mr. Warren drew Deborah close by his side and wrapped an arm around her. "Deborah Summers is the best thing God's brought to our lives since your mother, but you don't seem to have the good sense to figure that out. Why aren't you staying here and trying to win her, instead of acting like a man who doesn't have a lick of sense?"

Curt shook himself and straightened. "Didn't you read my note? I told you I was going to stop to see Deborah on my way out of town, and that I'd be back soon. I do love her, but from what I can tell the past few days, she doesn't feel the same." He grasped his horse's reins and patted his neck. "I heard what you told her a few days ago, that I'd leave her and not return this time. Apparently, she believed you."

Relief hit Deborah so hard she thought she might swoon. "So that's why you've been acting as though I don't exist?" She moved away from Mr. Warren and touched Curt's sleeve. "If you'd listened a minute or two longer, you'd have heard me tell your father I don't believe that, and that I care for you."

Curt's lips parted but nothing came out. "I'm so sorry. I'm ashamed I didn't give you a chance to explain." The words were mere whispers.

Mr. Warren shook his head. "Then you'd better ask her to marry you, boy. Women like Deborah and your ma only come along once in a lifetime. You let her go, you'll live to regret it." He scrubbed at his chin with his fingers. "I don't regret a day I spent with Sarah, but I do regret plenty of other days. I've not been the father I should have been to you."

He glanced at Deborah. "I stayed up half the night reading Sarah's journals. I'm ashamed of the pain I caused her all these years."

He turned his attention back to Curt. "And I'm ashamed of the way I've treated you, and all because of the anger I harbored against my own father. I made the nativity set for him for Christmas a year before I married your mother. He cut me deeply when he rejected my gift, and all these years I've taken it out on you, because you wanted to follow his chosen path rather than mine."

His gaze dropped for a moment, and then he raised his eyes and met Curt's. "I hope you'll be able to forgive this old man his foolish ways and accept something I'd like to give you both." He tapped Curt on the chest with his finger. "But first, do you plan on marrying this gal?"

Curt smiled. "If she'll have me." He took a step toward Deborah then hesitated and glanced toward the door. "Mrs. Summers? I need to ask your permission first. Would you do me the honor of allowing me to ask for your daughter's hand?"

Deborah pivoted, her heart swelling with delight as she spotted her mother's beaming face.

Ma walked toward them and stopped beside Mr. Warren. "I agree with your father, Curt. It's better late than never, and I hope she has the good sense to say yes."

Curt bowed his head then turned his attention back to Deborah. "I'm sorry I misjudged you. I've loved you for as long as I can remember. Like Pa said, I've made some foolish choices, but all that's behind me now. Would you make me the happiest man on earth and marry me?"

Joy spiraled through Deborah like a spring wind kicking up its heels in a grove of trees, setting the leaves to dancing. "I will, Curt. I love you, too. I always have."

He took her hands in his. "We'll make it work. I'll help take care of your mother and work your farm, if that's what you want. I'll even give up my woodworking. I plan to be a good provider, and I don't want to ever let you down."

Mr. Warren strode across the barn to a workbench covered by tack and other supplies. "You keep doing what God designed you to do, son, and you'll never let her down. Now, I hope both of you will accept this as a wedding gift—if you see fit to have it in your home, that is." He removed a large cloth to reveal the beautiful nativity set then stepped aside as she and Curt drew close.

A small gasp left her mother's lips, and Deborah glanced at her, noting a tear trickling down her cheek. Had Sarah shared her husband's pain with her mother and Ma had kept it a secret all these years?

Awe filled Deborah as she saw the pieces in the light filtering through the window above the workbench. Each one had been cleaned and polished until they shone with a burnished light. They were even more beautiful than she remembered.

Curt breathed out an exclamation of wonder. "You made these, Pa? They're exquisite. I've never seen such fine craftsmanship." He gazed at his father as he cradled a figure in his hands. "This is the finest wedding gift I could imagine."

Tears welled in Mr. Warren's eyes. "You truly think so? My pa told me they were no good, and I believed him. I was younger than you were when you went away, and I decided never to touch wood again, other than hammering a board across a stall or building a crate for storage."

As the four stood in reverent silence gazing at the nativity, Deborah looped her arm through her mother's, and Curt put his arm around her shoulder and his other hand on his father's shoulder. "I agree with Curt. This is a precious gift, and one we'll treasure forever. And it will look perfect at our wedding, if Curt wants to marry me on Christmas Day."

Curt turned adoring eyes on her and whooped. "You'd marry me next week? That soon? Don't you need to make a dress?"

She shook her head. "I've always wanted to wear Ma's dress. It fits me perfectly, and I love it. This nativity will be the centerpiece on a table at the front of the church, and that's all the beauty we need, besides our love and that of our families." She stood on tiptoe and kissed Curt square on the lips then blushed and peeked at Mr. Warren. "That is, if you don't object to us marrying so soon."

Curt stiffened beside her, but Mr. Warren chuckled and threw his arms around them both, drawing them into a hug. "I feel as though my soul has gained peace at last, and a Christmas wedding sounds perfect to me. Don't just stand there, boy. I'll unsaddle your horse while you kiss your bride-to-be."

About the Author

Miralee Ferrell and her husband, Allen, live on eleven acres in Washington State. Miralee loves interacting with people, ministering at her church (she is a certified lay counselor with the AACC), riding her horse, and playing with her dogs. An award-winning and bestselling author, she speaks at various women's functions, and has taught at writers' conferences. Since 2007, she's had ten books released, both in women's contemporary fiction and historical romance. Miralee recently started a newsletter, and you can sign up for it on her website/blog.

The Snowbound Bride
by Davalynn Spencer

I have set the Lord always before me: because he is at my right hand, I shall not be moved.
PSALM 16:8

Chapter 1

Spruce City, Colorado
1885

Arabella Taube clutched her small carpetbag as tightly as her breath and turned her back to the coach car. The man in the brown bowler had watched her all the way from Denver. He was watching her now through the window. She was certain of it.

Blowing snow swirled around her skirts, and the cold nipped at her ears. Oh, to have her trunk and be off to the hotel with the other passengers. She rubbed her jacketed arms as couples claimed their baggage and trudged through the snow toward waiting hacks and buggies. With this delay, there might be no rooms left when she got there.

Stomping her freezing feet against the platform boards, she looked again for a porter. She had assumed the train would press on to Leadville without stopping for the night. *"Assumption is the devil's joke on the unwitting."* Her grandmother's brittle warning chafed, and the woman's disapproving *tsks* rang in Ara's ears. Or was that the pop and snap of the engine as it cooled?

Horses whinnied and tossed their heads as they pulled from the station. She stiffened against the bluster of wind and panic. She *would* make her own way without her uncle's ordering of her every step and Grandmother's resentful regard—as if Ara could go back and change her parentage. The train heaved a dying breath, and the engineer stepped from his cab. The conductor followed. Where were the porters with her trunk?

The brown-bowlered man exited the car, looked both ways, and skimmed over her as if she didn't exist. She was not fooled and turned quickly for the depot. An inside bench would serve if need be, but she'd not be ogled by that man any longer.

The fine hairs on her neck sprang like porcupine quills. He was following her. *Ladies do not run.* She lifted her skirt and quickened her pace. As she neared the depot door, the clerk reached for the shade. Casting off Grandmother's drill, she ran and grabbed the brass doorknob. "Please," she mouthed.

He shook his head, jerked a thumb over his shoulder, and dropped the shade. The light dimmed within, and she turned to see the bowlered man a few paces away, lighting a pipe. The flare of his match lit pale eyes that watched her askance. Her stomach knotted. She didn't know his name, but she knew he was one of her uncle's lackeys, one willing to do for a price what her uncle would not.

Well, she'd not be bullied back to Chicago to be sold as a bride to the highest bidder. Uncle Victor could solidify his latest business alliance some other way. With tight resolve, she raised her chin and walked calmly toward the end of the building. At the corner, she turned and ran, skirts a-flying, to the nearest wagon. Tossing in her bag, she grasped the side but stopped short at the bared and snarling teeth in her face.

A scream lodged in her throat, but she scuttled to the harnessed horse where she dared draw in a desperate breath. A dinner biscuit from her skirt pocket abated the nag's nervous whinny. "There now, old girl," she whispered, her voice betraying her racing heart. A velvety nose rippled over her shaking hand, lipping up the broken bread. "You wouldn't give me away, would you?"

Pulling in great gulps of cold air, she spied the dog watching her from the wagon bed, head cocked and sharp ears pointing.

She dug in her pockets for another bribe, but

found only a hanky and a paper with the name of the Leadville banker she was to contact upon her arrival. She had to get her belongings, guard dog or no.

Easing closer to the board, she sent up a silent prayer and cooed at the beast. It seemed to warm to her voice and laid its ears down. The tail wagged. "Good boy you are, guarding your master's wagon. Might I retrieve my bag, please?"

Suddenly the dog crouched and turned from her with a chilling growl as the brown bowler came round the depot. Ara dropped to her knees and crawled under the wagon. Pipe smoke pinched her nostrils, and her chest seized.

The mongrel lunged against the side boards, drawing uncivilized expletives from the man's throat and distance from his feet. In his fright he dropped his pipe and stooped quickly to retrieve it. Ara feared she'd been found out, but he showed no sign of spotting her and fled the area, leaving a trail of curses behind.

Returning to its previous position, the dog waited quietly for a moment then rumbled a low beckoning. Ara crawled out, peered into the shadows hugging the depot, and slowly straightened. Brushing off her skirts, she spoke again in soft tones.

"You old love. If I had another biscuit, I'd let you

have it for sure." Afraid to pet the animal, she eyed her bag so foolishly thrown into the wagon before she knew what else was there. "Will you let me get my things?"

The ears flattened again and the cur smiled, if that was possible. But in Ara's unsettled condition, she believed—and hoped—anything was possible and made for the back of the wagon.

Black-and-white paws matched her steps and stopped by the carpet bag.

"There's a good boy. I'll just be taking my—"

The dog clamped upon the handle, dragged the bag to the center of the wagon bed, and sat protectively beside it.

"Well, I never!" Narrowing her eyes, she drew herself up. "I'll not be had by a dog."

A slight woof puffed from the pointed snout.

"We'll just see about that." She marched around to the wheel, yanked her skirts above her knees, and climbed the spokes. The dog looked away as if scandalized.

Ara stepped into the bed and froze as mangled strains of a Christmas carol rose from the alley, coming her way. She glared at the dog who again seized the handle in its jaws. With no other recourse but to leave her belongings and risk running into her uncle's shady minion, she dove to the rough boards, flattened against the outer edge, and jerked a loose tarp over her feet and head.

"God rest ye merry, gentlemen, let nothing you dismay—"

She clapped her hands over her ears. *Dismay, indeed. Have mercy!*

The dog howled then shook the wagon as it bounded to the edge.

"That bad, ol' boy? I don't sing any worse than you."

A muffled woof and exuberant wiggling indicated its master had returned. A decided tilt as the man climbed to the seat threatened to roll Ara like a Yule log from her hiding place. Whoever he was, he was either rotund or robust. At least he wasn't the brown bowler.

With a light slap and a hearty "giddyap, ol' girl," the mare took to the road. Ara sucked in a dusty breath. Should she rise and call out? Demand the driver take her to the hotel—where there may be no rooms? What if her uncle's hireling was watching? With a drawn-out groan, the dog settled its warm body against her. O Lord, what had she gotten herself into?

Chapter 2

Nate Horne bunched his shoulders and pulled his hat down. A ground blizzard would drift what snow they already had at the ranch and close the road he traveled. He called Beetle, but the dog didn't respond. A quick glance found it curled against a tarp, tail wrapped round its nose like a squirrel in a knothole. Nate reached back and rubbed the speckled ears and re-counted the crates and barrels he'd taken on at the mercantile before going to supper. He roughed the dog's side with hearty approval. It'd sooner take a man's hand off than let a thief steal their stores.

He didn't recall, but whatever lay in the tarp would be frozen before he got home. Just like him. Thanks to all the train passengers, he wouldn't be staying at the hotel as planned. Rooms had disappeared like cabbage in the chicken yard.

"Get on girl. No sense dragging it out." The wind cut cold against his face, freezing his lashes. He pulled his neckerchief over his nose and ducked his head.

Atop the first of many hills into the back country, a hearty gust cleared the air for a spell and a black vault opened above him, sparkling like a diamond-littered canopy. The spectacle took his breath away—that and the muffled sneeze from the wagon bed.

Beetle didn't sneeze like that.

Nate eased off the road and set the brake. He tucked his coat flap behind his holster, settled a hand on his gun, and stepped over the seat. Beetle flattened his ears and looked away as if caught chewing the tablecloth from the clothesline again. Nate waved him off, and he slunk to a corner, guilt painted all over his mottled face.

The gun slid smooth, and the cold hammer click spurred movement beneath the tarp. "Out." He raked his eyes the length of the roll, searching for the business end of a gun. Something squirmed, then stilled. At the top, the canvas tucked down, and a woman's green hat peeked out, followed by two enormous dark eyes. "Stand up."

Gloved fingers tugged the tarp under a pointed chin. "But it's s–s–so cold."

"Now." Relieved to see the rest of her clothes matched her hat and not some saloon gal's get-up, he eased the trigger back but kept the gun trained. He'd heard about women with derringers in their skirts or handbag or wherever. His neck warmed as a few wherevers piled up at the back of his mind. "Drop the tarp and show me your hands."

She complied and shivered against a hard-hitting gust. He waved the gun toward the seat. Looking away while she maneuvered over the bench, he met the dog's reproachful glare. "I'll deal with you later," he said under his breath. It dropped its head and grunted down on its front paws.

Nate holstered his gun. "Scoot over."

She scooted. He sat on her right, keeping his gun from her reach. As tall as she was, if she'd a mind to wrestle him for it, she might put up a good fight. He had never hit a woman—or knocked one out of a wagon—and he didn't want to start tonight. He pulled the tarp over the seat and handed it to her. "It'll be a couple hours before we get to the ranch, and you'll freeze to death in those fancy riggin's."

Her eyes grew even bigger. "Two hours? Ranch? But I must stay in Spruce City!" Her teeth chattered as she stood and wrapped the tarp around her like a squaw, then hunched on the seat next to him.

"Closer to three, and we're not turning back."

She blinked, and tears bunched up in her eyes.

"Quit that or your eyes'll freeze shut."

She stared at him, rubbed her face with gloved

fingers, and jabbed out her chin. "They will not."

"Suit yourself." He gathered the reins, released the brake, and clucked Rose on. They'd be even later now.

❦

Ara had read about ranchers out West. They all wore spurs and chewed tobacco and slurred their speech. Of course, she'd kept her dime novels well hidden from Grandmother and Uncle Victor—beneath her unmentionables. And when she left, she'd tucked them into her trunk.

Her trunk. Would she ever see it again? Would she ever make it back to Spruce City and on to Leadville? She'd given her word to arrive mid-November. She turned to the stranger whose face was swathed in a knotted neckerchief and nearly hidden beneath a wide-brimmed hat. "We have to go back."

He grunted and kept driving. It was like talking to the dog.

"Please, I have to be on the train tomorrow morning. I'm meeting someone in Leadville."

He slanted her an eyes-only look she'd expect from a bandit. What kind of person had she attached herself to? She snugged the tarp tighter and squeezed her eyes shut against the wind. How foolish she'd been to toss her bag willy-nilly into an unknown wagon, and then herself. She'd been so desperate to elude the bowlered man that she'd let go of her wits and now bounced along next to a horrific singer who draped himself like a Bedouin. A sudden jolt shot her eyes open. Snow danced in swirling eddies against the wagon and across their path.

"Badger hole."

Another jolt knocked her against the man's shoulder, and she jerked back. His eyes slid her way. "I won't bite."

Looking over her shoulder, she envied the dog snug and content in its thick coat.

"But he might."

The stranger did not laugh outright, but she heard it in his tone. How dare he.

"What were you doin' in my buckboard?"

She gritted her teeth. Could she trust him? She peeked his way, allowing that he hadn't put her out along the road to die from the cold or Indian attack or some other unthinkable fate. "I was trying to get my bag."

He turned in the seat, searching the wagon's contents. "What's it doing back there?"

"Your dog dragged it to the center where I couldn't reach it."

Another shaded look. "And how did Beetle get it?"

Beetle? What an odd name for a dog. "He dragged it there."

The man pulled his neckerchief over his nose and mumbled something behind his hand. She was certain he'd sworn.

"You put it in the wagon?"

She pressed her lips together and tugged the tarp higher. "Yes."

He leaned closer. "What?"

She leaned away. "Yes. I put it there."

"Look, ma'am, you'd best tell me what's going on 'fore we get to the ranch. It'll make a difference in what happens once we get there."

In spite of the *ma'am*, fear shot straight from her frozen backside to the roots of her elegantly pinned hair.

Chapter 3

Nate looked at the woman hunched beside him. "What's your name?"

She turned her big doe eyes on him. "Ara."

It sounded like *air-uh*, like a breath. "Ara what?"

She hesitated. If she said Smith, he'd know she was lying.

"Taube. Arabella Taube." The panic had dimmed.

He slid her another look. She started battin' her eyes again. No wailing, just a small jerk with every silent sob. Finally, she pulled the tarp over her green hat and buried her face in her hands. Hang fire, he could sober a bawlin' calf but not a crying woman, not even his own ma. What was he supposed to do with this one?

Something deep inside him wanted to wrap her in his arms and hold her close. He gripped the reins tighter. Not happening. He'd as soon rope a rattler than tangle with a female who misunderstood his intentions.

A fat flake dropped on his knee and quivered into a wet spot. He raised his head and another fell on his face. The clouds had dipped low and thrown open their shutters, about to empty their load.

⸎

Numb all over except where she slept against him the last hour, Nate pulled up in front of the ranch-house steps. He'd tucked the gal under his arm to keep her from sliding off the seat, and she'd murmured but didn't rouse. She fit against him as if she was made special order for his long, lanky frame. Leadville, she'd said. Maybe she was some rich man's bride-to-be, but tonight he'd make sure she was warm and safe.

A shadow crossed one of the two front windows, and the wide door swung open. His ma hurried out, wrapped in a quilt and holding a lamp. "You're home." The wind snatched at her words.

He ducked his hat against the snow and tied off the reins. "Out," he told Beetle, and the dog flew over the wagon boards and into the house. His ma leaned from the top step and held up the lamp. As gently as lifting a newborn foal, Nate scooped Ara into his arms, stepped down with a slight jostle, and carried her inside, tarp and all. His ma followed and shouldered the door closed.

A glowing fire warmed the parlor, and he laid his bundle on the settee.

"Is she hurt?"

The cold knots in his back and legs kinked tighter as he straightened. Moving to the fire, he rubbed his hands together and turned to warm his back. "Not far as I can tell."

"Where'd she come from, and why did you bring her out here in a blizzard?"

"I didn't know she was in the back of the wagon till she sneezed."

His ma raised an eyebrow.

"She rolled herself in the tarp. By the time I heard her, we were too far out to turn around." He backed closer to the fire and flexed his shoulders in the warmth. "The hotel filled up with train passengers, or I'd be in town, too."

His ma held the back of her hand to the woman's forehead. "Do you know anything about her?"

"Said she was on her way to Leadville to meet someone. But I'll be danged if I know why she threw her satchel in the wagon. Said Beetle wouldn't let her get it." He rubbed his hands over his head and down his face. "Maybe you can get more out of her."

"Did you get her name?"

"Ara Taube."

His ma's hand drew back and her voice dropped

to a whisper. "Taube? She must be German."

He added a log to the fire and poked around it until it flamed. "You're up late. Is everything all right?"

She set the lamp on a small table and pulled a footstool close to the settee. "We're all fine here. Buck went to bed hours ago. But I knew you'd be home." She patted her chest.

Nate couldn't count the times his ma had "known."

"I'll take the wagon and Rose to the barn. The stores'll keep for tonight." He glanced at the mantel clock about to call the hour. "Be back 'fore long." He hitched his collar up, called the dog, and ducked into the wintry blast as the New Haven clock began to chime.

⁂

Ara bolted upright at the striking tones. Her heart jammed her throat, and she clutched at the tarp. The culprit perched on a broad mantle above a roaring fire. Where was she?

"Hello."

Startled, she jerked around to a kind-eyed woman with a smile as warm as the hearth. Relief weakened her shoulders, and she slumped, waiting for her heart to find its way back to her chest.

"I'm Nate's mother, Lilly Horne. You're at our

ranch, and this is my home."

Nate? The wagon driver? "P—pleased to make your acquaintance." Ara cringed. This was no social call. "I mean. . . ." She fingered her hat, askew on the side of her head, and held out her hand. "I am Miss Arabella Taube. From Chicago."

Lilly's eyes brightened, and she took Ara's hand. "Oh, it's been so long since we've had guests. I do hope you'll stay awhile and visit. There's so much I'd love to hear about. The latest fashions. The theater—" She swept Ara with a worried look. "Please forgive me. Here I am thinking only of myself." Standing, she helped Ara rise. "Let's get you out of this dirty thing. Land sake, look what's it's done to your beautiful velvet suit." Crumpling the dusty tarp in her arms, she continued. "Oh my, but that deep green is absolutely lovely against your dark hair."

Ara sat again. The tarp soon found its way to the door, and Lilly pulled the small quilt from her shoulders and draped it over Ara's lap.

"I have a kettle on the stove, and I'll be right back with a cup of tea." She paused at the door to the kitchen. "You do drink tea, don't you?"

Ara tugged the fingers of one glove. "Yes, ma'am. Thank you."

The woman's smile broadened, and then she hurried through the door in her trousers.

Chapter 4

Ara blinked. Lilly Horne was wearing britches.

The second of her gloves joined its mate on the cushion, and Ara laid aside the quilt. Gingerly standing, she tested her legs for balance before moving closer to the fire. With her back to the luscious warmth, her stiff joints relaxed, and she took in the cozy room. Log walls bore lovely paintings of forested landscapes, and above the mantel hung a portrait of a dark-haired man astride an exquisite horse. A large desk sprawled beneath one wide window, and as she watched, snow built up on the sill, reminding her of the long cold ride. But she didn't remember arriving.

"Here we are, dear." Lilly brought a tray to the small table.

Ara returned to the settee, and Lilly took the footstool rather than one of two large leather chairs. With a warm smile, she handed Ara a delicate cup and saucer. Such contrast. A woman in trousers crouching on a stool serving tea in fine china. Beautiful artwork covering rough log walls, and a blazing fire dispelling the cold of a stormy night. Somehow it all seemed so natural.

"The paintings are lovely."

Lilly appeared pleased. "Thank you." She lifted her gaze to the portrait above the fireplace. "I haven't done much since Nathan passed."

Heavy footsteps on the porch jerked Ara's attention to the door and her cup rattled on its saucer. Had the brown-bowlered man found her?

"Don't worry." Lilly touched her hand. "It's only Nate dusting the snow from his boots."

With a whoosh, the door flew back. Flurries raced over the threshold to die in the entryway. Beetle darted in, and the stranger followed with Ara's carpetbag in hand, looking for all the world like a fairytale giant. She'd not realized earlier how big he was. Freezing to death had been more on her mind than appraising his stature. He set her bag against the wall, hung his coat and hat on the hall tree, then pulled his boots off in a metal jack that looked like a large beetle. That couldn't be where the dog got its name.

A cold nose touched her hand, and she sloshed her tea. Beetle eyed her, that odd grin tugging his jowls, then he trotted to the hearth and curled into a ball.

The driver passed behind her, smelling of leather

and snow. A dark wool shirt hugged his broad shoulders, and the scarf still circled his neck. Without his hat, blond hair fell across his brow, and bright pink tipped his ears and nose. He stood with his back to the flame, and blue eyes swept her with bridled appreciation. He nodded once.

Rattled by his obvious assessment, she returned his nod as curtly as possible. She could be just as tight-lipped as he.

Lilly chuckled. "Nate, Miss Taube is from Chicago. I'm hoping she'll stay awhile as our guest and bring me up to date on the latest happenings in the city."

Not wanting to offend her hostess, Ara quickly arranged her refusal. But not quickly enough.

"She'll be staying." He looked toward the window. "Storm's comin' hard. We'll all be staying."

Ara's heart leaped back to her throat. She sprang from the settee, spilling tea on her skirt, and rushed to the window. Ice lashed the pane like tiny claws across a hardwood floor, and the drift on the sill swept twice as high as before. Cupping a hand to her face she leaned against the glass but saw only swirling white assailing the house. Tears stung her eyes, and she gritted her teeth, determined not to appear childish and ungrateful.

A log gave way, and the fire crackled. Beetle sighed heavily, but the Hornes remained silent. Straightening, she faced them. At last she'd fled her uncle's dominance, only to be held hostage by the weather, a captive houseguest of a family she knew nothing about in a wild and mysterious land.

Oh Lord, if only I had wings like a dove, for then I would fly away.

❧

Nate rolled his shoulders and stretched his neck. The gal's hair lay knotted on her shoulders, and the fine dress was smudged from being wrapped in that old tarp. He still wanted to wrap his arms around her.

His ma rose from the stool. "Come stand by the fire, dear. You'll catch your death over there by the window."

Nate stole into the kitchen for coffee he knew would be waiting. Cradling a tin mug in both hands, he returned to the parlor door. Ara slumped on the footstool near the fire, staring at the copper flames. The hat shared the table with the teapot, and his ma was working through the tangled hair the same way he'd pulled cockleburs from a mare's mane one spring.

He pressed his fingers to his thumb, felt again the prickly burs that itched for days. His uncle had laughed at him for not wearing gloves. Next time he did.

She looked at him then, those doe eyes filling up her face. He moved closer to the fire and gentled his voice. "You hungry?"

"I set a plate in the oven for you, Nate. There's enough to share between the two of you." His ma spoke quietly, intent on untangling that mess of brown mane. He returned to the stove, grabbed a towel, and pulled out a tin platter heaped with beef and potatoes and carrots. He scraped some onto a plate and added a fork and napkin. She was probably a dainty eater.

When he returned, her hair hung smooth and shiny over her shoulder and pooled like dark water in her lap. "Thank you, Lilly." Weariness edged her eyes and voice.

His ma patted Ara's arm and handed her the pins. "My pleasure. Always missed having a daughter to fuss over." She stood, took one of the plates, and handed it to Ara. "Though Nate here kept me plenty busy, growing out of his clothes faster than I could make them." She pulled the leather chairs closer to the fire so each one angled toward the warmth and gestured for Ara to take a seat in one. "Do you have more than the satchel Nate brought in, dear?"

"My trunk is still on the train." Easing into the nearest chair, Ara sent Nate a worried look. "What do you think will happen to it?"

He took the other chair, ducking her pleading eyes. "They'll offload it in Spruce City or take it on to Leadville."

"And then?"

She made him feel responsible. "They'll hold it." He forked in a mouthful.

Ara relaxed against the high leather back, fitting to it like she'd fit beneath his arm.

"Morning will be here before we know it." His ma smoothed her hands down the front of her britches and picked up the lamp. "Your room is on the right as you go down the hall, Ara. Mine is across from yours. Just knock on my door if you need anything. I'm a light sleeper."

Ara laid down her fork and gave his ma a weak smile. "You've been very kind."

As his ma left the room, darkness leaped into the corners where the fire's light didn't reach. Ara stiffened and gripped her plate with both hands.

He leaned toward her, close enough to hear her quick, shallow breaths. Softly he spoke, like he would to a jittery colt. "It's all right. You're safe here." He had a need to touch her, but he held back.

She turned her head, and the fire glinted off her dark eyes like a flame against obsidian. He'd seen that look before.

"I'm not afraid."

He returned to his meal, determined not to argue the point. Arabella Taube might not know it, but she was scared to death.

Chapter 5

Sparrows twittered, water dripped, and a dove called, insistent in its beckoning. Ara rolled to her side and burrowed into the warm feather tick. Her elegant bed in Uncle Victor's mansion could not compare. Hoping to see the same log walls that had housed her for a week, she opened one eye, then offered a silent *thank-you*. Somehow, the Hornes made her feel wanted.

It's all right. You're safe here. Nate's deep, soft words spun a tight coil in her stomach each morning when she rehearsed them. He'd tried to ease her worries—quite unlike his frightening demeanor on that dreadfully cold ride. He was different here in this house. No longer the cloaked Bedouin or masked bandit, his very presence commanded safety. And next to him and his mother, Ara felt less the gangly giant that towered over others. She fit in.

But she was far from where she needed to be, and Lilly had seemed to understand when Ara explained she'd taken a position as a private tutor for a Leadville banker's children. Even Nate and Buck had nodded mutely at that dinner conversation. Everyone knew that when the snow melted enough for the wagon's passage, she'd be on her way to Spruce City and the train.

A part of her dreaded that day.

She tossed back the quilt and tiptoed across the cold floor toward the incessant dripping. Beyond the heavy lace curtain, icy rapiers clung to the eaves, pouring themselves one drop at a time into tiny pools beneath the window. A sapphire sky spread over the mountain-rimmed valley, and the brilliant landscape shone like a blue willow dream. Eyes aching, she turned from the window with Nate's warning in her ears. "Don't stare at the snow. It'll blind you." She squeezed her eyes tight and drew in a crisp breath. Winter was so different here. In Chicago all was gray for weeks on end.

And the tall horseman was different from any man her uncle had pushed upon her. Had she met Nate Horne in the city, she might never have left. A wrenching shiver sent her to the foot of the bed where a blue calico dress and two flannel petticoats lay over the footboard. More of Lilly's kindness. That first morning the woman had brought black coffee on a tray. Her blue eyes smiled over her cup brim, and she pulled Ara in with a motherly gaze.

"From the size of that satchel, I imagine you don't have another change of clothes, and your traveling suit is ruined. Would you accept something from me to wear for the time being?"

Embarrassed, Ara considered refusing. But what choice did she have? Lilly took the dress and petticoats from a chest against the wall. "I wore this dress the day I met Nate's father, and I saved it back for my daughter." The last word faded with a shadowed pause. "It's been packed away so long it has creases where it shouldn't." The simple style and fabric spoke of a young woman not well-to-do by any means.

"It's lovely." Ara took the dress and held it against her breast. "You wore it when you met Nate's father?"

Lilly picked up the tray. "I was a mail-order bride and wore that dress on the train, all the way from New York." A sad smile drew the corners of her mouth. "Nathaniel Horne met me at the Spruce City depot with my picture in his hand and a promise in his eyes."

Ara's heart pinched at the thought of such risk, but from the look on Lilly's face and the sprawling log house, their marriage must have worked out for the best.

"Those were wonderful years, and the good Lord blessed us with Nate."

Who, with his uncle, ate nearly as much as the foaling mares kept close in the barn, Ara had since learned. The rest of the horses and a few cows wintered beneath the mountain.

Shedding her gown with a shiver, she stepped into the petticoats and dress again, flouncing the skirt over the warm flannel layers. Lilly had worn nothing but britches since Ara arrived. What might that be like?

∞

Nate drove the team into the barn, and Buck unhitched the sled. Haying the horses took near all morning after they bogged the runners. At least the band was close, on the south side of the mountain. He pulled the heavy harness from the Clydes and led them to their stalls. A good brushing, a can of corn, and a pile of hay paid them for their labor. A pitchfork full to Coffee one stall over, and Nate paused to run a keen eye over the bay's distended belly, ready to drop any day. She whiffled her thanks as she nosed into the sweet grass, her long, dark neck as smooth as Ara Taube's eyes. Coffee-black and lit from the inside out, they were. Longing sneaked in and curled around Nate's heart like Beetle near the fire.

It'd only been a week, but if he could, he'd take

Ara in his arms and beg her to stay. Then he'd ride out, whistle up a bear, and make a winter coat from its hide. He huffed at the likelihood of either prospect.

The close warm air splintered with a sudden crack. Buck lifted the ax and moved to the next bucket in line down the alleyway. "It's thinner this mornin'. Too bad we can't keep this ice for summer when your ma makes lemonade and we're sweatin' like the Clydes."

Nate grunted in agreement.

His uncle paused and tugged on the galluses holding up his pants. "That little gal seems to like it here."

Nate tossed a fork of hay and shot him a look.

"Your ma was hummin' in the kitchen this morning." Buck's ax rang through the barn like a rifle shot. "I ain't heard her hum in years. Not since your pa died."

Nate kept his thoughts to himself.

"You think a city gal would take to the high country?"

He ignored the question, moved on to Rose, and rubbed between her ears. She tossed her head and blew warm air in his face. No foals for her, but she'd earned her hay.

"Lilly's bakin' cookies today." Buck set the

buckets in the stalls, hefted the ax to his shoulder, and grinned beneath his wide brim. "Think I'll go in and help her out with 'em." His whiskered face bubbled on the sides. Made Nate laugh every time.

He hung the fork on the wall. "Be right behind you. Need to check a couple things first." Like what he was going to do around Ara Taube until the road was passable. In a short week he'd grown partial to her gentle ways and lively eyes. He'd like her to stay, forget about Leadville. A frozen knot in his belly thawed at the notion. He dug through a box of rawhide and horsehair bundles, hoping he could untwist his thoughts by twisting *mecate* reins or building a headstall. He felt near loco thinking about her.

Beetle woofed at him.

"It's all your fault."

The dog looked away.

"If you'd scared her off like you were supposed to, she wouldn't be here, and I wouldn't be feeling like I had hot coals in my chest."

The dog grinned. Nate snorted and headed outside.

Chapter 6

At the porch, Nate stomped his boots and side-stepped Beetle as the dog skedaddled through the front door. He shed his coat and hat, scrubbed his hands through his hair, and smoothed his mustache. Anticipation had him all bowed-up. Laughter snagged him like a dried thistle bush and pulled him to the kitchen, where his ma was taking cookies from the oven. Buck and Ara sat at the table drinking coffee, and Beetle laid at Ara's feet, the turncoat. As Nate stepped through the doorway, his ma laid a pan of gingersnaps atop a towel on the table. Then she knifed under each one to loosen it from the tray. His mouth watered like it had when he was a boy.

Caught in conversation, Ara looked up with a laughing smile that melted like a pale sunset the moment their eyes met. His chest tightened. She dropped her gaze and pushed at the braided twist of hair at her neck. Buck caught the sudden shift and cocked a ragged brow at Nate.

But his ma chattered on. "Take a seat, Nate. My brother is going to get most of them if you don't scoot to the table."

He grabbed a cup from the counter and straddled a high-back chair. Buck poured the coffee, and his ma flipped a cookie in the air with her knife. Nate snatched it and watched Ara's eyes and mouth go round with surprise. His ma flipped one to Buck, paused with a look at Ara, then flicked one her way. To her credit, Ara caught it and laughed aloud. The sound shimmied up Nate's back and down his arms like cool rainwater. Dunking his cookie in the coffee, he leaned over to take a bite.

Ara's brow pulled down. "Do you always dunk your cookies in your coffee?"

"Don't you?"

Buck choked trying to hold back a laugh.

"Ara, I must apologize for the men of this house. They've always dunked my gingersnaps. My dear Nathan taught them his atrocious manners, and living way out here in the high parks, I couldn't see any point in spoiling their fun."

Ara dunked her cookie but it broke in half and sank.

"Like this." Nate repeated the move. "In and out." Then he popped the softened part in his mouth.

She mimicked him, grinned with her success, and puckered her lips around the bite.

His pulse bucked and ran. Wanting to run himself, he went to the parlor to check on the fire. By the time he returned, his uncle was gone and Ara was pouring hot water in the sink while his ma scraped the cookie sheet. He stopped at the doorway.

"Your family seems to enjoy one another." Ara set the coffee cups in soapy water, then unbuttoned the cuffs of her blue dress and rolled up the sleeves.

His ma chuckled and shook her head. "A merry heart is medicine indeed. It's so much easier to laugh and joke and carry on. I can't imagine living any other way."

Ara pushed a rag inside the cups and nearly washed the color clean off.

His ma looked over her shoulder. "Is it different in your family?" The question came out quiet and gentle, in that way she had of getting at the truth.

Ara sighed. The blue fabric stretched across her back as she drew in a deep breath. "Yes, very. That's why I'm on my way to Leadville. Trying to start a happier life on my own."

Nate turned on his heel and made for the front door with Beetle close behind. He had to get outside, away from that tall, slender woman who wouldn't leave him be, whether he was drowning in her dark eyes or trying to drive her from his thoughts.

But it was hopeless. He was already roped and snubbed to the post.

⌒∞⌒

Ara had fallen easily into the rhythm of ranch life. She rose early to help Lilly with breakfast, listened without blushing as the men talked about the latest foaling, and decided once and for all that Nate hated her.

He kept darting off to complete some chore rather than remain in her company for any time at all. And he had every right to hate her. She had stowed-away in his wagon, won over his dog, barged into his family, and was traipsing around in his mother's dress. Not that Ara had any choice over what she wore, but resentment was a bitter and familiar enemy. She didn't want to be the cause of anyone else's gall, but there wasn't one thing she could do about her situation other than set out on foot for Spruce City.

But that was no longer what she wanted.

She placed four dripping cups on the counter, and a heavy sigh escaped before she could stop it.

Lilly touched her arm. "Leave those, and come sit. I need more coffee."

The woman clearly ran this ranch just as Grandmother ran Uncle Victor's household, but with a far gentler touch. Ara dried her hands on her borrowed apron and took a seat at the table, cradling the cup Lilly had refilled.

"Tell me what troubles you." Lilly swirled her coffee, looking into its depths, leaving Ara free to speak without scrutiny.

Avoiding her suspicions about Nate, Ara chose the safer of two troublesome thoughts. "I gave my word to Mr. Lancaster that I would arrive before the holidays and take over his children's education. Yet here I am, snowbound far from the train and unable to even send a telegram. He must think I've gone back on our agreement."

Lilly's eyes shadowed with worry. "Is it so bad here?"

Remorse flooded Ara's heart and burned her cheeks, due retribution for a partial truth. "Oh, please, that is not what I meant. You have been nothing but kind to me."

Lilly reached across the table and patted her hand. "Don't fret, dear. The Lord tells us to let Him take care of the things we can't. And we can't do a thing about the weather."

Mutinous tears crowded Ara's throat. "This is all my own foolish fault for hiding in Nate's wagon. For not showing myself and begging him to take me to the hotel as soon as I knew he was a good man."

With motherly pride, Lilly leaned in. "And when did you know my Nate was a good man?"

Now it was Ara's turn to stare at her swirling coffee. She'd not even admitted the truth to herself. "As soon as I heard him sing."

Lilly sputtered and covered her mouth. Ara squirmed with embarrassment.

"It's a wonder his singing didn't send you running in the opposite direction." Lilly shook her head and her eyes crinkled shut with laughter. "You should hear Buck. He's worse. I don't know how Beetle stands it when they ride out after the mares. All that cater-wauling."

"I did cover my ears, but his tune was less of a threat than the man following me."

The news stilled Lilly, and a sharp line formed between her brows. "Do you know who he was?"

"He's one of my uncle's henchmen, sent to drag me back to Chicago. Uncle Victor had his own ideas of whom I should marry, but I chose not to accommodate his business dealings."

Flushing with anger, Ara gripped her cup tighter. "That's why I hid in Nate's wagon." The surface of her coffee rippled. "I'll not be traded like chattel."

Chapter 7

Wind licked the mountain's summit, and snow danced up like white dust devils. After a month of alternating cold and snot-slick thaws, the weather's siege appeared to be over. Ara Taube might be on her way back to town. Out of Nate's sight and out of his life. And he'd go plum out of his mind longing for her. He leaped onto the porch and reached for the door, but it opened on its own, and he nearly stepped on his ma's boots. His eye ran the length of sheepskin coat and found Ara peeking over the collar. It still caught him off guard.

"Beg pardon." Habit shot his hand to his hat brim.

"No—it's altogether my fault." She clutched the scrap can with a smaller tin inside it and peered at him with her big brown eyes.

His insides turned to marmalade. "You huntin' the chickens?"

She nodded. "Lilly said they're in the back of the barn."

The gal had set her hand to every other household

chore. Might as well see the coop. "Come on."

She followed him off the porch and along the sloppy path to the barn, where she plowed into him when he stopped at the doors. "Oh!" Her breath puffed out like a new heifer's.

He tipped his head back and squinted at her.

"I know," she said with a deep sigh. "I'm not to stare at the snow. But it's so beautiful, I can't help it."

Neither could he. He dragged his eyes from her perfect lips. "No smoke stacks."

Curiosity lifted her brow. "You've been to Chicago?"

"Shipped some horses there. Rode along on the train." He unlatched the barn door and held it open for her. "I saw enough."

Curiosity gave way to judgment, and her brows dipped. "You make it sound like a horribly disgusting sight."

"Truth is—" The words caught in his teeth. It wasn't her fault he didn't take kindly to crowded streets and close-packed buildings.

She held out the small can. "Truth is you like it better here." Her voice dropped. "So do I."

Shocked by what he thought she'd whispered, he thumbed his hat up a notch and took the can. "You do?"

She walked inside and switched leads without a stumble. "Lilly said you can make a star-shaped cookie cutter out of that tin."

"I can."

She moved deeper into the barn. "The chickens back here?"

He led her to the back of the barn and held the wire gate open while she tossed in the scraps, then pulled it shut. "We open that wide door to the outside yard when it's not so cold."

Curling her fingers through the mesh, she watched the chickens scrabble. The top of her head came to his nose. He leaned toward her to catch a whiff of her hair. She noticed.

He jerked back.

"I won't bite." She tipped her chin toward the chickens. "But they might." With a wry smile, she left him standing by the coop holding an empty peach can and a bucketful of foolish.

⟡

The next storm frosted Ara's window with fern-like patterns and bound her to the house. She and Lilly did nothing but cook for the men, who did nothing but shovel snow and feed horses. Dreams of Leadville faded as if they belonged to someone else, and tallies in the back of her Bible marked off four-and-a-half weeks. She'd never been happier.

In the kitchen, Lilly punched down a creamy mound of bread dough, puffing yeasty goodness into the air. She folded two smooth loaves into baking pans, smeared butter on each top, and set them on the back of the stove. Then she wiped her hands on her apron and went to the small pantry off the kitchen while Ara peeled potatoes for dinner.

"I imagine it will be hard without your family this year at Christmastime."

Ara's mouth went dry with distasteful memories of Christmas in her uncle's mansion. Cold. Formal. Forced. Slicing back the tight skin, she peeled away her family's facade. "Not really."

Lilly returned with canned green beans, strawberry preserves, and a face full of curiosity. Ara accommodated her.

"I was as much a decoration in Uncle Victor's home as the towering tree he insisted upon each year. Something to flaunt when his associates came to parties. I abhorred them."

"His associates or the parties?"

"Both."

Lilly gathered her apron in hand and took hold of a jar, twisting against the tight seal.

"Grandmother saw to it that I was properly

schooled and churched, but I learned at an early age that she resented me."

A choking noise fell from Lilly's lips, and she sloshed bean juice down her apron and onto the floor as the lid gave way. Ara reached for a towel.

"Lately these jars are a fight." Lilly turned aside and swiped her face with the back of her hand. "I do believe they're sealing tighter, or else my hands are getting older." She pulled a thin smile across her lips.

Ara stooped to mop up the water. "Let me help you."

For a moment, Nate's eyes looked out from beneath his mother's graying brow. A longing washed over the woman's face that shot an unnamed ache deep into Ara's chest.

Lilly gathered herself, set out a large skillet, and filled it with strips of salt pork. "We'll add onions and the beans. It's Buck's favorite." She checked the fire and situated the skillet. "What of your parents?"

Heat licked Ara's face like fire beneath the cast-iron. Would she never be free of her past? Halving the peeled potatoes, she took a deep breath. "My mother died unwed in childbirth. She was Grandmother's only daughter, and I was hers."

Ara filled a kettle with water, added the potatoes,

and waited for judgment to stab with a pointed remark or a disgusted *tsk*. Instead, a breathy "Oh, my" followed her explanation. Pity was as distasteful to Ara as resentment. She moved the kettle to the stove and prepared for the onslaught.

Lilly sliced an onion into her skillet. The pork sizzled. "That explains how you ended up on the train to Leadville alone." Not a speck of disapproval seasoned the woman's words, as if Ara's background made no difference at all. Ara's brow relaxed and cooled, and condemnation drained from her heart like the water she poured off the green beans.

Chapter 8

By the time dawn blushed the sky, Nate was dressed and holed up in the barn, looking for peace in the familiar scent of horseflesh and hay. Lantern light haloed the stalls as he fed, and Coffee greeted him with a deep rumble.

"I see she's done tangled your spurs."

Buck's sleepy voice rolled down the alleyway, and Nate turned to see him leaning against the doors, daylight licking his boot heels. Nate grumbled a greeting.

"That kinda talk ain't gonna win her."

Nate flexed his grip on the pitchfork. "I don't know any other."

Buck ambled to the corn bin, scooped out a can, and gave it to the Clydes. "Sure you do. Just tell her how you feel."

Nate jammed the pitchfork into the ground. "What if she doesn't feel the same?"

An honest stare drove his uncle's point marrow-deep. "Would you be any worse off than you are now?"

Nate made for the door and tromped across the frozen mud to the chopping stump. The smooth ax handle in his hands and the snap of the splitting log helped ease the burn in his gut. And if that burn didn't let up soon, they'd have enough firewood for three winters with some to spare.

An hour and half-a-row later, a hearty mix of steak, potatoes, and coffee lured him to his seat at the table. Ara set out the serving dishes, and her arm brushed his shoulder when she drew back. He cut his ma a look to see if she'd noticed fire sparking on his sleeve, but she took her seat smug and satisfied as a milk-fed cat, holding her hands out for prayer. Ara's soft fingers slipped into his, and he bowed his head as Buck said grace. No calluses on Ara's hand. No cuts or rough edges. Could she survive on a horse ranch in the Rocky Mountains, or would she resent him for filling her life with hard work and worries?

A canyon stretched between holding her hand and asking for it.

"Nate, have you got a cookie cutter for me yet?" His ma's question startled him, and he dropped Ara's hand. Buck coughed and helped himself to the fried potatoes.

"Almost." Regretting the lie, Nate knifed a slab of beef and tried not to look guilty. He hadn't even started on it.

"Good. Christmas is only ten days away, and Ara and I have plenty of baking to do. Buck, have you seen any promising trees yet?"

"Saw a little bunch at the mountain's base when we hayed the mares."

"Good. I'd like to get our tree up early this year since I have help decorating." Her eyes sparkled like tinsel when she looked across the table at Ara. "You men won't be bothered."

Buck drooped his face like a hound pup. "Now Lilly, you know I was countin' on helpin' you put those doodads on the tree again."

"I'll remember that, little brother."

Nate concentrated on his beef, washing it down with hot coffee.

"Did you see the trees, Nate?"

He glanced at his ma and nodded, grateful for a full mouth.

"Good."

That was her third *good* in less than two minutes. Something was up.

She snagged Buck again. "And you're still working on the new crèche I asked for, aren't you?"

"Yes, ma'am. Got a fine piece o' willow and started Joseph last night."

"Will you have all the pieces finished before Christmas with all the other chores you have?"

Nate filled his mouth. There were hardly any chores at all other than shoveling snow and mucking out stalls. He shot Buck a look in time to see something pass between him and his ma.

"We can't have missing pieces in the crèche. It wouldn't be right." Without so much as a sidestep, she collared Nate. "Why don't you cut the tree today? Take Ara with you. It would do her good to get some fresh air, and we may have only one clear day before the next storm hits."

Ara's fork stopped in mid-air the same time as Nate's, and they both stared at the innocent-looking woman at the head of the table.

"I've got some old trousers I think will fit you just fine, Ara. We'll get you bundled up good, and I'll trust you to pick the best tree for the parlor. Can't be taller than Nate, though, to fit in the corner by the window." She gave Ara a winning smile and completely ignored her son.

Buck took great interest in buttering his bread and kept his head tucked. Nate couldn't see his mouth, but his whiskers twitched. That was a dead giveaway.

Chapter 9

The denims scuffed when Ara walked across the bedroom, and she giggled behind her hand. Grandmother would be scandalized. But the trousers didn't chafe as she'd expected, and already she was warmer in the wool shirt and belt that held everything together. The thick socks Lilly had given her weeks ago were now comfortable old friends, as was the sheepskin coat she wore almost daily.

After her initial embarrassment dissipated at breakfast, Ara found herself giddy with anticipation. She could not have planned a better outing. This time, Nate couldn't run off without her. And she would know for sure if he hated her or felt the same tug in his heart as she.

Or maybe he felt nothing at all.

The cold thought ushered in a more worrisome concern: she'd never ridden astride. If she fell off and broke her arm or leg, it would be even longer before she was fit to take the train to her promised employment. Guilt wagged a pointed finger at her as Ara wrapped Lilly's red scarf around her throat. Instead of riding out to find a tree for the parlor, she should be riding into Spruce City to send a telegram.

Boots stomped onto the porch, and she took one last look in the hall-tree glass. Beneath the wide-brimmed felt with her hair tucked up, she could pass for a boy. The door swung open, and Nate's presence consumed the close entryway and most of her breath. "You're ready."

She raised her chin to his typically abrupt statement. "Of course."

His eyes snapped with amusement, but he didn't laugh outright. Lucky for him, for this morning, dressed as she was and near as tall as he, she felt certain she could set him down.

"Come on then."

Would he ever speak to her in more than three words? Warmth spread through her chest at the thought of one three-word phrase she wouldn't mind hearing.

Rose and another horse stood tethered to the front porch railing. Nate stopped next to the mare. "Grab the saddle horn with your left hand and the cantle with your right."

Stunned by the lengthy explanation, her eyes followed as he touched each part of the saddle.

"Then put your left foot in the stirrup and pull yourself up."

Gripping the horn that looked nothing like a horn, she did as he said. For once, her height proved a definite advantage. Rose danced sideways.

"Relax." Nate pulled her foot back until only the front rested on the stirrup. "Keep your heel down." He stepped around and repeated the process on the other side.

"Why?"

Blue eyes squinted up at her. "You want to get dragged?"

She gasped and gripped the horn with both hands.

"Relax," he said again, but gentler. "Rose can feel your tension. The boot heel will keep your foot from slipping through the stirrup." He pulled the reins from the railing and looped them over Rose's head. "Hold these in your left hand. Don't pull back unless you want to stop."

Evidently, Nate Horne didn't mind talking about horses. Gathering his own reins, he mounted, leaned forward, and patted his horse's neck. "Badger will lead." A near smile tipped his mouth. "Do what I do." With that he turned toward a snowy peak across the valley.

Rose didn't follow well. Ara tried to relax, but the mare trotted to catch up, pounding Ara's teeth and body with each jolting step. At last she settled alongside Badger in a more relaxed gait. If Ara were a gambling woman, she would bet Nate was silently laughing.

❦

Ara was no horsewoman, but she had promise. Nate imagined her riding the high parks with him, becoming confident enough to help drive the mares down. This was what he'd been missing—someone to be his partner other than Buck. And someone who was easy to talk to as long as he wasn't looking at her. As they cut across the open valley side by side, her dark eyes and perfect mouth didn't distract him. He huffed and shook his head. Half the morning she'd had him dishing up more words than he'd used in a month.

"Have you always lived here on the ranch?"

He slid her a look. She was taking in their surroundings and sat a little easier.

"Don't know anything else. Pa started with that sorrel stallion in the portrait over the fireplace. High Park King." He patted Badger's neck. "Direct descendant here."

She eyed his mount. "Shouldn't his name be

Prince or Duke with King for a sire?"

Nate laughed. "Too sissified."

She looked straight at him and cocked one brow. "And King isn't?"

"Nope." He held back a grin trying to figure her next comment.

"What happened to your pa?"

Danged if she didn't get right at it. He swallowed a sharp pain in his throat and reined Badger around a gnarled cedar stump. "A horse fell over backward with him. Broke his neck."

She gasped and jerked on the reins, but Rose ignored the impulsive tug. "I'm so sorry."

Her comment was to be expected, though *sorry* didn't cover what he'd learned to live without the last twelve years. "I've been as long without him as I was with him." He reset his hat, squinted at the mountain. "Buck moved in after the accident. Helped Ma and me with the ranch and just stayed on. He's got a good head for horses."

As they neared the mountain, evergreens flaunted their heavy robes among the naked aspens. Any of a dozen young trees would suit the parlor. Nate pulled up.

Ara stretched her back and neck. "I'll probably hate you and Rose tomorrow."

Her comment jabbed a fearful dart, but he held his tongue, stepped off Badger, and dropped his reins to the ground. Ara threw her leg over then buckled beneath her own weight.

He reached for her arm. "Give yourself a minute to get your land legs. You'll be sore, but it'll wear off."

She grimaced and rubbed one thigh. "It's not that I don't believe you. It's just that I highly doubt it."

He laughed outright and impulsively reached for her hand. "Come on. You need to pick a tree."

Chapter 10

Ara's heart sang. Nate didn't hate her. His spontaneous grasp was as good a proof as anything, and nearly as perfect as the tree she chose.

After he felled the spruce, he tied off the bigger end and looped the rope round his saddle horn. Then he returned the hatchet to his saddle bag, loosed a tarp from behind his saddle, and spread it on a snowless patch away from the horses. "It's too cold to stay long, but we might as well eat sittin' as ridin'."

Ara knelt on her heels, her stomach threatening to consume itself. Nate dropped cross-legged in the opposite corner and unrolled the bundle between them. Sliced bread and roast and cookies made up the fare. She'd never tasted better.

Nate drank deeply from a canteen and passed it to her. The water was cold and sweet. "Thank you," she said, handing it back.

He smiled as if relieved she'd accepted his offer, twisted on the lid, and laid the canteen beside him. Then he pushed his hat up and rested his arms on his knees. "What do you think of this country?"

Disappointed that he wouldn't speak of something besides the scenery, she held in a sigh and scanned the horizon, admitting that it had no rival. "It's magnificent. I had no idea the Rocky Mountains were so breathtaking."

He rumbled a wordless response, apparently pleased that she appreciated the raw and rugged terrain as much as he did. Leaning back on her hands, she boldly stretched out her legs and squelched a vision of Grandmother coming down with the vapors. A blue swath spread above them, jays sassed from the near trees, and the horses nibbled at bare spots in the snow. Chancing a look at her companion, she found him as majestic as the land on which he lived—strong and tall and silent. Like the stand of dark pine on the mountain that braved harsh storms, he survived on his own, and she admired him for it. A sorrowful heat filled her chest. His loss was greater than hers, for he had known and loved the parent he lost. She had not.

"I didn't know my parents, but I can imagine the pain of losing a father you so admired."

He flinched ever so slightly, as if she'd touched a bruise, and fingered a hole in the tarp. "Your uncle raised you?"

At last—a personal question. "With his mother, my grandmother."

He glanced up from beneath his hat brim, and his eyes flashed like the darting wing of a blue jay. "Why'd you leave?"

Ara chose her words carefully, not wanting to spoil the moment by speaking too intimately. "Uncle Victor arranged a business deal contingent upon my marriage to the other party. I refused."

He grunted and worked his jaw with obvious disapproval.

"I was running from his hireling when I dared to hide in your wagon." The confession brought his eyes to hers, and he held her gaze for a long silent moment. A question dangled in the air. He cleared his throat and fiddled with the tear, working it bigger with his finger. His nervousness sparked her own, and as he worried the tarp, an unseen thread tightened between them. She tucked her fingers beneath her legs to keep from slapping his hand from the growing tear.

He cleared his throat again and shot her a look. "Could you live here?" He frowned and his hand jerked back, ripping the hole farther. "I mean, do you still have your heart set on going to Leadville and teaching that banker's young'uns?"

Breath froze in her lungs. Of course she could live here, but what did he mean? Stay on the ranch and help his mother or stay in Spruce City as a teacher? Or something else? Her heart began to pound, and she tucked her feet beside her and folded her hands in her lap. "I made a commitment to tutor Mr. Lancaster's children."

Nate smoothed his mustache and mumbled under his breath. She leaned toward him expectantly. "Excuse me?"

He slid her a quick look. "If you liked it well enough here on the ranch, I thought you might want to. . ." Again he mumbled and looked away.

She leaned closer, forcing him to face her, and tried to hear what he wasn't saying. "Might what?" If he had intentions toward her—and she hoped he did—he'd have to put them into words. She needed to know if he was looking for a ranch hand or a wife.

He huffed out a breath and looked her straight in the eye. She held his gaze, and her heart thrummed with anticipation. Yes, he was a man of few—hardly any—words, but three would do if strung together in the right order. Suddenly he jumped to his feet and towered over her, his hands working like billows. She stood as well, a spiny tingle ringing her neck and running down her arms on fiery feet. The heat in his eyes left no doubt. But instead of coming for her, he stooped and made quick work of the tarp, rolling it into a tight bundle, remains of their lunch and all.

"Sorry 'bout that." He pulled his hat down and strode to his horse where he retied the tarp behind his saddle and mounted. Badger danced in a circle, proving a horse does indeed sense its rider's distress.

Deeply embarrassed, Ara looped the reins over Rose's head and attempted her earlier success at mounting without assistance. But now she fumbled and could not pull herself and her heavy heart into the saddle.

Nate leaned from his saddle, grabbed her around the waist from behind, and hefted her up. She looked to catch his eye, but he turned away. The rope tightened on his saddle horn, and the beautiful blue spruce dragged behind them with a scolding swoosh as they rode wordlessly back to the ranch.

◈

Ara would never accept him after the dust-busting he'd just put her through. Hope had risen like mist in the morning, but Nate said something wrong or didn't say something right, and now that hope had burned off, leaving him dirt-dry and empty. From the corner of his eye he caught her stiff back and shoulders, that pert chin squared out over her hands. She was right. She'd hate him and Rose tomorrow. Him more than Rose.

Daylight was running the ridge by the time they reached the barn. Without a word, Ara jumped down, tied the reins to the rail, and politely thanked him for the ride and lunch. Then she walked away and left him standing with his heart in his hands and a tree tied to his horse.

Chapter 11

Ara made it to her room and managed to shut the door with a quiet tick without alerting Lilly. Throwing herself across the bed, she buried her face in the feather pillow and pounded her fists on the ticking. She wanted nothing more than to stay on the ranch with Nate. But he hadn't even professed affection, let alone love. She could have had that kind of marriage in Chicago.

And what of Mr. Lancaster's children awaiting their teacher? *O Lord, what am I to do?*

"Don't fret," Lilly had said. Ara growled into the pillow. How not to? Pushing herself up, she rubbed her face, then went to the washstand. Tepid water stood in the pitcher, and she filled the basin and bathed her face and neck and hands. Then she changed out of the denims and put on Lilly's calico. She didn't even have her own clothes. The least she could do was wear her own worth.

Freshened, she drew her Bible from the nightstand and sat on the bed. The thin pages fell open to her favorite psalm, and she read the words aloud, as much from memory as sight. " 'I have set the Lord always before me; because he is at my right hand, I shall not be moved.' " That's what she needed—to not be moved from her goal. But was tutoring in Leadville the Lord's goal for her? Had she answered Mr. Lancaster's ad simply to escape her uncle's dominance?

"O Lord, have I made a mess of things?" She rubbed her temples and thought back over her path to the Hornes' ranch that seemed only a series of missteps. Had God been directing her? She looked again at the familiar scripture, and it soothed the ache, just as it had countless times when Grandmother blamed her for her mother's death. Ara truly believed she was never alone, but she longed for something more, something she feared she might never have. Closing her eyes, she whispered a prayer for guidance. If the storms cleared and the ground dried enough, perhaps Buck would drive her to the train.

Revived and encouraged, she returned her Bible to the nightstand and marched down the hall and into the parlor. Lilly held the tree, and Nate lay half hidden beneath its branches, tightening the screws of an iron tree stand.

"Ara, you outdid yourself. It's beautiful." Lilly's

face shown like the angel atop Uncle Victor's enormous tree in the great hall. "Tonight we will pop corn over the fire. I have cranberries saved in the root cellar, and when Nate finishes the star cutter, we can add sugar-dusted cookies."

Ara's brave plans melted like butter on warm bread. She could no more leave now than fly to the rafters, for she refused to dampen this generous woman's Christmas. Mr. Lancaster surely had other resources, a man in his position. And how much studying would two eager children accomplish anyway so close to Christmas? The Leadville banker would simply have to wait.

That evening Ara strung fluffy corn and red cranberries and lost more blood from pricked fingers than she'd thought possible. Even Nate set aside his muted manners and joined the festivities. But Buck kept his distance in the corner, where he sat whittling a figurine, gathering the shavings to toss on the fire and twitching his whiskers every time she caught him watching her.

In spite of the tension with Nate, Ara had never known a Christmastime as warm with Grandmother and Uncle Victor. With a twang of sadness, she doubted they knew such a family hearth was possible.

The next morning, Nate's neck and shoulders cramped like a froze-up well pump. His belly felt full of prickly pear, and even his fingers itched. He sat on a stump at the barn, soaking up borrowed sunlight and making a set of short ties for Ara's hair. They'd be her Christmas gift if she didn't refuse 'em like she'd refused him.

"Didn't go so well?"

Nate's hands stilled, breaking his rhythm, and his heart dropped to his belly. His uncle read sign like he was tracking a six-toed lion. The man came up from behind, leaned against the wide door, and pulled a figurine and his knife from a pocket. Nate frowned and went back to twisting the red and gray hairs into a pattern. These heart-to-hearts were rubbin' a sore on his temperament.

After a few fumbles, his hands fell against his thighs, and he blew out a heavy breath. "I figured she knew. That look she gets when she takes in the land—I thought she'd like living here with me."

An extra-long piece slid from the willow. Nate tied off the hair, set it aside, and rubbed the back of his tight neck. Then he stood and kicked the stump he'd been sitting on.

"Don't spit the bit now, son. She's not gone yet."

Nate stashed his work and beat it outside, scratching at the stinging itch in his fingers. He couldn't reach the one in his heart.

Chapter 12

Anticipation hung in Ara's heart like diamond icicles, sparkling and pure. Cradled as they were on the breast of the mountain, glitter and glamour didn't fill the house. Instead the special care given to selected recipes and homemade gifts graced this home. The scent of cider and cinnamon and cloves curtained the kitchen, and star-shaped cookies winked from red yarn on the popcorn-and cranberry-laced spruce.

She shrugged into the sheepskin coat and tucked the denims into her boot tops before making her way to the barn with the scrap can. Another snowfall had chased her out of the calico and into the borrowed britches.

Just inside the barn's wide door, she paused by a new wooden manger filled with fresh hay as if awaiting a heavenly guest. Bending to breathe in the grassy perfume, she closed her eyes and marveled at the simple pleasure. A scuffling step said Buck was near.

"It's an offering." He stopped beside her and fluffed the hay with his large, rough hands. "He came to stockmen, you know. Like us. And His ma made His bed in a barn."

Ara's heart warmed at Buck's uncharacteristic tenderness. "It's a wonderful gift. Exactly what the Christ child would need."

His thick brows rose with hope. "You really think so?"

"Of course. Warmth and shelter and love. The same things we all need. I'm sure He would have been most comfortable in this crib you've made."

A smile puffed out his whiskers, and Ara swallowed a laugh. Such pleasure in a modest gift made from what one had at hand.

Her gifts would be far less than modest, for she had little else but her efforts to give this generous family come Christmas Eve. If there were enough dried fruits in the larder, perhaps a stollen each? Her stomach fluttered at the idea of giving Nate a part of herself, even if only her labor. She longed to give him more.

At the barn, she tossed the kitchen scraps to the hens and watched them vie for the choicest bits. Once she'd stopped scraping and scratching over Leadville, peace had settled in her heart. Worry did not help clear the road or ward off the storms. Nor did it get her to the Spruce City depot. What a waste to miss all the joy of the season worrying about something over which she had no control.

Returning along the alleyway, she stopped to visit each mare and foal. Three had delivered beautiful, long-legged youngsters since she'd been at the ranch, and Ara delighted in the mother-and-child atmosphere that filled the barn.

A shadow suddenly darkened the doorway, and a man stood backlit against the sun. The breadth of his shoulders and the line of his hat brim gave him away. Her breath quickened. "Good morning." She smiled, hoping he would join her at the stable's half door to watch Coffee with her baby.

Nate came to stand beside her, smelling of wood smoke and leather. His gloved hands folded over the edge of the door as he regarded the dark brown mare and her foal. "Named him Bean."

Laughter burst out before she could stop it, and she covered her mouth. The tilt of his mustache said he'd intended the joke, and she admired his wry wit. "With those gangly legs, it's a wonder he can stand at all."

Nate huffed a brief laugh. She'd grown accustomed to his silent conversation. No wasted words, no foolish prattle. Just a deep and quiet presence. She would miss it.

He looked at her, and she listened with her eyes for what he was thinking and feeling. Her pulse thrummed with what she thought she saw in the way he held his mouth and the intensity of his blue gaze, but his words stilled the song.

"Ma wants greenery for the parlor."

She let out a deep breath. "Well then, we'd best be at it."

Following him into the deep snow toward a clump of trees, she spared herself some effort by stepping inside his large footprints.

"Take the small branches from the bottom." With a quick twist and snap, he jerked off the tender shoots and cradled them in his arm. Ara had no gloves to protect her from the prickly needles and sticky sap, but she bent beneath the spreading boughs and broke off what she could.

Watching Nate ahead of her, surrounded as they were by pillowy snow, she gave into a childish urge. Laying her few short branches in a neat pile, she formed a large snowball from stiffer, melting snow, stood up, and took aim. The missile hit him in the neck, and he stopped. Delighted yet terrified, she muffled a shout with icy fingers. He slowly faced her with heat in his eyes and a curl in his lip that she took for a playful threat. Or was it real? She turned and ran.

His first round hit her squarely in the back of the head, knocking a gasp from her lips. She ducked, but not before a second snowball pummeled her and then a third. Feeling as mature as Coffee's colt, she took cover behind a wide spruce and began amassing ammunition. During a brief lull in Nate's barrage, she counted eight snowballs in her cache. Snow crunched behind her, and she turned with a cry.

Like a hat-wearing grizzly, Nate lunged, knocking her into her carefully piled snowballs. The sound of his laughter set her heart free, and they tossed fistfuls of snow at each other until they fell together, exhausted by their battle. He elbowed himself up and leaned over her, his eyes simmering, his quick breath close and warm. And then he pressed his warm lips against hers.

Everything she'd ever wanted pulsed with the heartbeat of this mountain horseman. He drew slowly back and searched her face, his cheeks as red as a robin's breast. Then he offered his hands to help her stand. Unable to contain herself, she threw her arms around his jacketed waist and laid her head against his shoulder.

"You're shivering."

With delight. "I don't have my gloves."

He removed his. "Take mine."

Christmas Wedding Bell Brides

She slid her fingers into one unmanageable leather casing. "They'll never work. You keep them."

"I'll get yours." He cupped her cheek with a hand, and she leaned into his warmth. "Wait here."

She nodded and shivered anew when he left her side and trudged off through the snow. Did he know where to look? Stepping forward, she raised her head to call after him, but a different gloved hand clamped across her mouth and nose, cutting off her voice and breath. She fought to free herself, but an arm circled her waist and threw her onto the snow where again her mouth was covered with a smooth doe-skin glove. Her muffled scream and clutching fingers drew a snarling leer across the man's face.

How had he found her? And where was his brown bowler?

Squirming beneath his weight, Ara sank her teeth into the fine leather. He jerked away with a curse. Ara filled her lungs with the burning cold of mountain air and split the sky with her scream.

Chapter 13

Nate's heart and footsteps froze. That was not a playful taunt. Terror cut through the forest beyond the ranch house, and Nate turned and charged down the path he'd just made. Coyotes? A cougar? What had drawn that blood-chilling cry from Ara's throat?

He shouldn't have left her, should have carried her to the house. His hands balled into stony fists as he crashed through the trees, jerking to a rough stop at the sight of a man holding Ara by the waist with a gun at her temple.

"Stop or she's done for," the man yelled.

Hurt her and you're bear bait.

Nate's breath cut sharp into his chest, and his arms flexed defiantly as he forced himself still. He ached to feel the rough's neck in his hands.

Yellow teeth winked beneath a mustached sneer as the man began walking backward, dragging Ara with him. She clawed at his hand.

"You'll not be takin' another step," her captor shouted.

He must be the man Ara had told them about,

but how had he found her?

A movement in the trees snatched Nate's eyes to the left.

"Don't be tryin' to fool me with that old trick." The scoundrel laughed and squeezed Ara up against himself with a cocky grin. "I know there ain't no one out here but the two o' ya'."

He snickered again. "The lass thought she could fool me, too, but I saw her hidin' under the wagon. Took me a while and a bit o' silver, but I found her, and her uncle will be repayin' me kindly when I bring her home."

Helplessness clutched Nate like an iron spring trap. He spread his open hands waist high to show they were empty. "Don't shoot."

"I won't if I don't have to, but if I do, the second bullet is for you." On the last word, he pointed the muzzle at Nate. Beetle leaped.

Sharp teeth pierced the thug's gun hand, and a cracking flash sent a bullet thudding into a tree. Ara broke away and fell to the snow, scrambling on her hands and knees.

Screaming and cursing, the man dropped the gun and pounded his other fist into Beetle's head. The dog didn't weaken but shook the man's hand as if to tear it from his body.

"Call him off! Call him off!"

Nate grabbed the gun and leveled it on the frantic fellow. "Down!" Both Beetle and the man dropped to the snow. Nate slapped his leg, and Beetle ran to him, human blood reddening his lip. Nate held his eye and aim on the weeping man and stooped to pet his dog. "Good boy, Beetle. You've earned your keep today."

⸎

The clearing snow that allowed the bully to reach the ranch also allowed Nate and Buck to haul him back to town trussed up on his horse. Ara insisted she ride along so she could wire Mr. Montgomery and check on her trunk.

At the depot she eyed the telegraph operator, recognizing him as the man who wouldn't let her inside on that blustery night so long ago. She wanted to kiss him for his stubbornness, but he was startled enough by her trousers. Instead, she described her trunk and asked if it had been left at the depot. He checked a list of unclaimed items, then took her to a small storeroom. Relieved to find it stacked with other forgotten baggage, she drew an earnest promise from him that he would hold it a few days more. Then she dictated a brief apology to Mr. Lancaster regarding her formerly stranded state. She wished him well in finding another tutor, but pressing matters prevented her from taking employment with him.

Matters like her heart that pressed against her ribs every time a certain lanky horseman looked her way.

She paid for the telegram and walked the short distance to the jail where Nate and Buck were turning over their prisoner with a less than glowing report of his conduct.

∞

That evening after supper, Ara pulled on the familiar coat and slipped out to the porch. Countless stars blazed from one horizon to the other—fuller, brighter than any she'd seen in the city. A deep longing surged through her to make those stars her own from this vantage point, and a sigh slipped out in a puff of white as she tugged the wool collar around her neck. Her future was less certain than it had been upon her arrival at the ranch six weeks ago: no employment in Leadville, and no idea of what she would do instead. But peace had settled within her. She was free, her own woman, and the Lord was with her.

Like an ill-timed intruder, the memory of Nate's fervent kiss sent shivers up her spine. He loved her. She was certain of it.

The familiar creak of the wide front door turned

her head. Warm light silhouetted a man as he stepped outside. Ara hugged herself to keep her heart inside her chest, but her confidence dissipated in a frosty puff. Perhaps Nate had simply been caught up in the moment, and yesterday's kiss meant nothing after all. The fine hairs on her arms prickled as he approached, and his warm breath at her ear loosed a deep yearning.

"Cold?"

Before she could answer, his strong arms enveloped her from behind, and he whispered her name against her hair. "When I came so close to losing you, I knew I couldn't let you go."

She closed her eyes and tipped her head back, wrapping his arms in her own.

"Marry me, Ara."

As her heart rose to accept, it quivered on a disappointing note. Would he never say he loved her? She turned in the circle of his arms, clinging desperately to her fragile belief that he did. Reaching up she smoothed his mustache, then laid her hand on his chest, drawing strength from his steady heartbeat and resigning herself to his ways.

He looked out at the night, scanning the wide, sparkling band that stretched over the mountains. "Beetle knew it before I did, but he was right." His eyes returned to her, dark and solemn. "I love you, Arabella Taube."

Surprise, relief, and delight flooded her soul, and she threw her head back and laughed at those wonderful words. Pulling her closer, he caught her lips with his own. Her lips, her heart, and her life.

Epilogue

Ara tucked Lilly's note in her coat pocket and met Nate at the wagon for their run to Spruce City. Instead of handing her up, her scooped her into his arms and kissed her soundly before setting her on the bench and joining her there. She took a deep breath and gripped the seat. He may be a man of few words, but he knew perfectly well how to get his point across.

Beetle sat proudly in the wagon bed, and Rose pranced out of the yard as though confident of her errand—Ara's trunk, fabric for a wedding dress, and a preacher to do the honors. Nate wrapped his arm around her and tugged her closer, and Beetle bounded over the seat to plant himself beside her. Ara laughed aloud at Nate's scowl.

"I hear a war of words between you two."

Nate snorted. "He's too smart for his own good."

Ara gave the dog a quick hug. "Well I'm certainly grateful for him. He saved my life and yours."

Another snort. "I had the gent where I wanted him."

Rolling her lips to squelch her laughter, she regarded her black-and-white bench mate. "You've never told me how Beetle got his name."

Nate's mustache rose on a crooked grin. "He was a sneaky thing as a pup. Waddle up behind you like a beetle without you knowin' he was there." Blue eyes studied her with a twinkle in their corners. "Quite the watch dog."

Beetle woofed and tilted his snout higher, and Rose flicked her ears at the laughter that rang in the chill morning air.

By mid-afternoon they were home, Ara's arms full of bundled fabric and ribbon as she stepped through the front door of the sprawling log house.

"Back here." Lilly called from her room—a room Ara had never entered. She stopped at the threshold, awed by the paintings. In one, a woman and child stood in a meadow, and in another a small dark-haired girl sat in a swing beneath a large tree. Ara's heart broke with sudden memories of hushed words and shadowed smiles. Swallowing an ache, she stepped into the room.

Lilly looked up from her treadle sewing machine and caught Ara's expression. "Her name was Emily. Such a delicate thing." She set aside her sewing. "These paintings are how I imagine she would have looked had she survived that first hard winter."

"I'm so sorry," Ara whispered.

Lilly pressed her palm to her heart. "We loved Emily for the time she was with us, and I love her still." She rose and went to her bedside table and picked up a small, fabric-covered box. "Like so many parents who have buried their children in this vast land, I've entrusted her to the Lord's care."

Ara set her purchases aside and shrugged out of the heavy coat. Lilly reached for her hand and wrapped Ara's fingers around the box. "This is for you. I can't wait for Christmas Eve."

Ara warmed beneath Lilly's smile and thought of the burgundy silk cord and brocade she'd bought to make a small reticule for this gracious woman.

"Please, open it."

Ara drew off the white satin ribbon and removed the lid. Two porcelain doves perched on a polished wooden base, so lifelike that their unheard cooing hung in the air. She lifted them from their velvet-lined nest and glanced up to see joy brimming in Lilly's eyes.

Ara's throat tightened. "They are exquisite."

"Nathaniel gave them to me on our wedding day." Again her fingers rubbed a spot above her heart, and a youthful memory warmed her eyes.

"He said I was his fair dove."

"Oh, Lilly, this is too much—"

She shook her head, cutting off Ara's protest. "I have long asked the Lord to bring Nate a dove of his own. I just did not expect her to come in the back of the wagon."

Laughter eased Ara's discomfort and brought a light to Lilly's eyes. "You are that dove, Ara. I knew it the night he carried you in, wrapped in that old dirty tarp." Lilly swiped her cheeks with a quick hand. "I knew as soon as he told me your name."

Ara's breath caught. So accustomed to her German surname, she rarely if ever thought of its meaning. "Taube," she whispered. *"Dove."*

Lilly smiled and pulled Ara into her arms with a laughing sob. "The Lord brought you to us, Ara. He answered my prayers and brought my Nate a dove."

⌒∞⌒

On Christmas Eve's eve, Buck replaced the New Haven clock on the mantel with his hand-carved figures and arranged the pieces just so. Ara scattered cedar twigs and pinecones among them. When she finished, he pulled a handful of sweet grass hay from his pocket, gently lifted the sleeping figure, and filled the manger before returning the Babe to His bed. Ara linked her arm through Buck's and gave it a squeeze. "It's perfect. What a wonderful talent you have."

His whiskers puffed out, and his eyes twinkled. "That's not all I've got." From his shirt pocket he pulled a mistletoe sprig with red yarn tied round the end. Then he tacked it to the low beam between the parlor and the entryway and gave Ara a wink.

She laughed behind her hands and hurried to the kitchen. They would celebrate that night with wild turkey and stuffing, squash and beans, pies and cookies, and enough cider and stout coffee to serve all of Spruce City. And well they might, for on Christmas Eve after the service, Ara would wed Nathaniel Horne II.

⌒∞⌒

The next evening, the small church was alight with candles on the altar, the window sills, and small tables against the walls. Pine boughs and red ribbons adorned the pews and perfumed the air with promise. Ara and Lilly stood at the back as Nate and Buck took their places in front, dwarfing the dear pastor. Ara smoothed her creamy satin dress marveling at the delicate doves Lilly had embroidered on each sleeve and the white fur muff the woman had pressed upon her.

With a catch in her heart, Ara gazed at the

strapping cowboy who stood so straight and tall, like a mighty pine. Lilly touched her arm and placed a delicate kiss on her cheek. "Welcome to the family, Ara. The Lord continues to bless us."

Ara blinked away her tears. "Merry Christmas, Lilly."

At her cue, Ara stepped into the aisle and halted in surprise as the congregation rose and began singing "God Rest Ye Merry Gentlemen." Nate's face lit with delight, and he tilted his head back to join in on "tidings of comfort and joy." His may not have been the most perfect pitch, but his deep voice flooded Ara with exactly what the song declared—comfort and joy. As she gained the front of the sanctuary and stretched her hand toward the man who held her heart, Ara thrilled to know exactly what it felt like to fly on wings like a dove.

About the Author

Davalynn Spencer is the wife and mother of professional rodeo bullfighters. She writes Western romance and inspirational nonfiction and teaches writing at Pueblo Community College. She and her handsome cowboy have three children, four grandchildren, and live on Colorado's Front Range with a Queensland heeler named Blue. Find her at www.davalynnspencer.com.

Also from Barbour Books....

Heartland Christmas
Brides

White Christmas
Brides

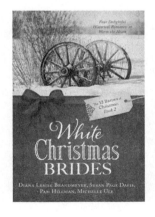